ONE KING OF A PROBLEM

ONE KING OF A PROBLEM
RISE OF THE GRANDMASTER™ BOOK TWELVE

BRADFORD BATES
MICHAEL ANDERLE

DISRUPTIVE IMAGINATION®

This book is a work of fiction. All of the characters, organizations, and events portrayed in this novel are either products of the author's imagination or are used fictitiously. Sometimes both.

Copyright © 2021 by LMBPN Publishing
Cover Art by Jake @ J Caleb Design
http://jcalebdesign.com / jcalebdesign@gmail.com
Cover copyright © LMBPN Publishing
A Michael Anderle Production

LMBPN Publishing supports the right to free expression and the value of copyright. The purpose of copyright is to encourage writers and artists to produce the creative works that enrich our culture.

The distribution of this book without permission is a theft of the author's intellectual property. If you would like permission to use material from the book (other than for review purposes), please contact support@lmbpn.com. Thank you for your support of the author's rights.

LMBPN Publishing
PMB 196, 2540 South Maryland Pkwy
Las Vegas, NV 89109

First US edition, November 2022
eBook ISBN: 979-8-88541-931-4
Print ISBN: 979-8-88541-932-1

Previously published as part of the megabook *The Eyes of Prophecy*

THE ONE KING OF A PROBLEM TEAM

Thanks to our beta readers
Kelly O'Donnell, John Ashmore, Larry Omans, Rachel Beckford

Thanks to the JIT Readers

Dorothy Lloyd
Veronica Stephan-Miller
Diane L. Smith
Jeff Goode
Allen Collins
Angel LaVey

If I've missed anyone, please let me know!

Editor
The Skyhunter Editing Team

LIST OF TIM'S CURRENT STATS AND SKILLS

"Tim" level twenty Hex Witch
  Primary Stats
  Strength: 14
  Endurance: 28
  Dexterity: 25
  Intelligence: 55
  Wisdom: 63
  Perception: 6
  Vitality: 4
  Revitalization: 4
  Luck: 7

Notable Gear
  Weapons
  Simple Dagger of Dexterity, +1 (X2)
  Greater Staff of Yin +3 Endurance +7 Intelligence +7 Wisdom
  Orb of Concentration, +5 Intelligence +4 Wisdom

Armor

Circlet of Divine Wisdom, +1 Endurance +3 Intelligence +5 Wisdom

Shoulder Guards of the Spotless Mind, +1 Intelligence +2 Wisdom +1 to Perception, Vitality, Revitalization, and Luck

Hex Witch's Armament, +2 Dexterity +2 Endurance +6 Intelligence +8 Wisdom

Jerkin of Fortuitous Solitude, +1 to all base stats, and bonus to healing when standing twenty feet away

Paul's Gloves of Mending, +7 Intelligence +4 Wisdom

Belt of Divine Inspiration, +1 Endurance +2 Intelligence +4 Wisdom

Hermit's Pants for Special Guests, +2 Endurance +2 Intelligence

Boots of Tranquility, +2 Endurance +2 Dexterity, Increase mana regeneration by 2%

Jewelry and Accessories

Leather Wraps of Divergent Health, 10% chance for single target healing spell to jump targets and heal the secondary recipient for 50% of the value

Wristband of the Faithful, +1 Endurance, ten seconds of double mana regeneration

Ring of Luminosity, +1 Endurance +2 Intelligence +3 Wisdom

Necklace of Hydration, +1 Endurance +2 Intelligence +5 Wisdom

Trinket of the Smiling Monkey, +1 to random stat

Skills

Curse of Sacrifice: Novice rank one
Hex of the Shattered Beast: Novice rank one
Appeal to the Goddess: Novice rank five
Night Vision: Novice rank eight
Quick Feet: Apprentice rank two

Rectify: Apprentice rank two
Disturbance: Apprentice rank three
Backstab: Apprentice rank four
Throwing Knives: Apprentice rank four
Sneak: Apprentice rank six
Shadow Master: Apprentice rank six
Small Blades: Journeyman rank one
Snare: Journeyman rank one
Dodge: Journeyman rank three
Flame Burst: Journeyman rank three
Behold My Power: Journeyman rank five
Divine Light: Journeyman rank five
Healing Storm: Journeyman rank five
Who Needs a Shield: Journeyman rank five
Curse of Giving: Journeyman rank eight
Cleanse: Journeyman rank nine
Healing Orb: Master rank one

Stances
Way of the River
Way of the Boulder

Buffs
Weaken Undead: Journeyman rank two
Armor of Eternia: Journeyman rank five
Attacks of the Faithful: Journeyman rank five

Open Quests
The Stone of Immoratis

CHAPTER ONE

Prince Desmond hovered over his father's bed, wishing he could do something to make him better.

The High Priest's adventurers failed on their first attempt to slay Isadora, but on their return through the crown's land, he'd sensed a great change in them. Since they rode past, he'd been by his father's side, waiting for the curse to break. It would be nice to end the day with some good news.

They had to succeed this time. They just had to.

"The duke is here to see you," the familiar voice of his manservant Thurstan called from the doorway.

Desmond looked down at his father's pale skin and wondered how much time he had left in this world. The man who raised him looked so frail, lying unconscious on the bed, but he would always remember his dad in his prime. They used to spend hours training and studying together. So much so that his mother put a firm stop to some of their shenanigans lest the kingdom suffer from his father's inattention.

He would never forget the times they snuck off to the city so his father could glean the heartbeat of the people. His father used to tell him that a wise king must not only listen to the nobles but the men and women working the land. The burden of keeping the kingdom running often fell on those at the bottom, and their voices mattered greatly to him.

No one cared for the people of Promethia like King Rasmus. He made sure that the crops got planted and the mouths of the hungry filled with bread. During his reign, the kingdom benefited from a stable peace with the desert kingdoms.

Peace was a wonderful thing. When they had it, the minds of men and women flourished. The arts and inventions that came out of times of great peace were the things Rasmus wanted for his legacy.

Thus the entire kingdom found themselves living in a golden age of magic and art.

While it was nice for the rest of the kingdom, the success of his father's rule put a great burden on Desmond. The prince spent most of his childhood knowing he had to be the best at every discipline to have even a chance of living up to Rasmus' legacy. How did one follow the greatest king in a hundred generations without looking like a blundering idiot? The last thing he wanted was for others to remember him as the king who squandered his father's hard work. He refused to be known as Desmond the Dummy.

So while other children played, he studied.

The one art he never mastered was politics. The art of lying to someone's face to get what he wanted eluded him to this day. His honor had cost him more than one friend, and the unyielding nature of his will burned even more bridges. It wasn't simply good enough for him to be the best.

He had to be better.

Desmond sighed. If the Duke was here, it could only mean trouble.

Keeping her waiting would only make whatever giant piece

of horse shit she was going to drop into his lap today worse. "Tell her I will be there momentarily."

"Of course, sir." Thurstan disappeared as silently as a ghost.

His mother rose from her chair, crossed the room, and clasped his hands. "Don't worry. I'll stay with him."

"I'll make sure this doesn't take long. I want to be here when he wakes up." Desmond kissed her on the cheek and dropped her hands.

He felt her eyes on his back as she called, "It takes as long as it takes. Make sure not to let her take advantage of you."

Of course, she was right. The duke was a strong-willed woman. Anyone should've been able to guess that by the way she claimed the title for her own. That didn't mean the duke could do whatever she damn well pleased. Her first duty was to serve the crown, and if that didn't happen more frequently, there would be dire consequences. The least of which was stripping the title she fought so hard for.

Walking out of the room was the only signal his two guards needed to follow. They trailed behind Desmond day and night whether he willed it so or not. It seemed with the king in ill health, no one was taking chances with his. What they didn't know was that the king would wake up soon. When Isadora died, the adventurers would have the cure, or better yet, her death would break whatever spell the king was under.

It just had to.

The guards entered the audience chamber with him and positioned themselves to either side of the door as he walked into the room. Duke Ravenstorm was sitting at the head of the table eating grapes off a silver tray and drinking a glass of wine. She could never make things easy. Everything had to be a power play.

Don't let her take advantage of you.

Desmond moved to the table and stood by his chair until she got up and moved to another seat. When she moved, the duke also sat in her new seat before he had the chance to claim his. So even in his tiny victory, she slighted him. Today wasn't the day to let it get under his skin.

Today was going to be a good day.

A small part of him wanted to give into the game completely and call her duchess when he addressed her. If she wanted to push the issue, he'd have her stripped of her lands and titles so fast that she'd be cleaning the chamber pots of a tavern by nightfall.

"What can I do for you today, Duke Ravenstorm?" Desmond poured a glass of wine.

This was going to suck.

"A carriage rode through my lands today, carrying the crown seal." Stephanie's body language looked bored, but her eyes were intense.

Desmond shook his head and set down his glass. Maybe drinking wasn't such a good idea right now. "You mean someone traveled through the lands you manage for the king while bearing his seal? I don't see how that's a concern of yours."

"It concerns me because the people riding in that carriage crossed my lands once without my leave already." She stared at him, daring him to correct her. "Last time, they carried the family crest of one of my men."

Oh, that must have really chapped her buns.

Desmond tried not to smile at the thought of a lowly adventurer having the guts to face down the duke. "This time as they crossed the king's lands, they carried a seal I handed to them personally."

He could play the power game as well as she could. The difference was that he was the one with all of it in this situation. As the acting king, his word was law. If he gave someone the royal seal, they acted with his voice and could go wherever the fuck they wanted. She was dangerously close to crossing a line.

Or maybe trying to get him to cross one.

"How am I to protect the crown when I don't know who is coming and going?" The duke leaned back in her chair. "It's almost as if you don't care what happens to the king." Her eyes moved toward the doorway he entered from.

This was why he hated politics.

This entire meeting was to set the stage for her trying to seize power when he became king. What Duke Ravenstorm hadn't figured out yet was that she would be crushed between three armies. He'd already promised her position to the marquess and the marquess' position to the earl. All they had to do was continue supporting him if it came to battle. Seeing sense in any given situation wasn't the duke's strong suit.

Desmond kept his voice even when he spoke, which under the circumstances should've earned him an award for best performance of the millennium. "Actually, they have the seal because they're heading to slay the witch Isadora. I wonder what kind of correspondence they might find there."

He played the card not knowing how close it would strike to home, but he instantly knew when it landed. Was she so stupid as to side with the witch over the crown? Maybe the real question was if it was ambition that drove her or something else.

The duke's eyes widened slightly at his remark. "Surely, I have no idea what you mean."

"If there isn't anything else, I have my father's recovery to attend to." Desmond took a small sip from his glass of wine.

The wine tasted like fruity piss in his mouth, but he swallowed it just the same. It was his nerves that were getting to him and not the quality of the wine. He was playing a dangerous game right now, but he was past caring. If his father didn't make it through the day, the first thing he would have to do was bring the duke to heel. So he might as well get a head start.

"No, I guess that's it." She rose and swaggered out of the room.

He was going to count that interaction as a win in his book. She'd slighted him at every turn, yet he found a way to make it through the conversation without losing his temper. Not only that, but he found out some useful information. He'd never considered her a direct threat, but now their cards were on the table. He was happy to have prepared for this day.

The only way they might avoid bloodshed now was if the adventurers found a way to save the king. He stayed seated for a moment drinking the wine whose flavor had only slightly improved. Appearances mattered. Even here in the heart of his castle, there were always eyes watching and gossip spreading. It wouldn't do his reputation any good to be seen storming away.

After finishing his glass, Desmond stood and slowly made his way out of the room. The guards followed him in lockstep until he made it back to his father's chambers.

His mother looked up from her seat by the bed. "No change."

"Damn it!" Desmond smashed his fist into his palm. "What's taking them so long?"

His first instinct was to pour another glass of wine, but with the duke lurking and his father's fate hanging in the balance, it was better to keep his wits about him.

Turning away from the wine bottle on the table, he focused his attention on his father in time to see one of his fingers wiggle. "Mom!"

The queen turned and grasped the king's hand in hers. "Rasmus, I'm here for you."

Desmond was standing behind her in an instant. "Me too, Dad."

ONE KING OF A PROBLEM

Slowly the king's eyes fluttered open, but the once faded blue was now slightly red. "Water," he croaked. "I need water."

Fully dressed and sitting on his throne, the king looked strong and hearty.

Watching him now, no one would've guessed he spent the last four weeks in a coma. His back was straight, and his head held high. There was a bearing of command Rasmus easily carried that Desmond knew he would never master in the same way.

He was so happy to have his father back, but there was also something wrong.

Rasmus wasn't acting like himself. Gone were his gentle ways. His normally jolly tone had been replaced with brusque efficiency as he issued orders. The red tint to his eyes still hadn't faded. This new version of his father was almost worse than having him in a coma.

No one could openly defy the king, not even his son.

"Father, before you retire for the evening, I have one last matter to bring to your attention." Desmond looked at his mother, and she gave him a slight nod to continue.

Looking down from his throne, Rasmus smiled. "For my son, I will always make time."

It sounded like his father and looked like his father, but Desmond wasn't exactly sure it was his father. Something was off. It could have been residual blowback from the curse, or maybe something else still had its claws in him. There was no way to know.

But he couldn't ignore it.

"There is the matter of the adventurers who slew Isadora and released you from her curse." Desmond lowered his head. "I promised them a reward from the treasury."

The king didn't look concerned. Their kingdom was wealthy enough he could afford to part with almost anything.

"What exactly did you promise them?" Rasmus' voice had an edge that didn't match the calm expression on his face.

This was going to be the hard part. It wasn't strictly in Desmond's power to offer the stone, but in times of dire need, it seemed a petty trinket. "I offered them the Stone of Immoratis if they could wake you."

"I'd rather have them killed!" the king bellowed as he rose to his feet. "What in the hell were you thinking?"

His mother tried to place a hand on the king's shoulder, but he brushed it off and marched toward his son until they were standing eye-to-eye. "That stone is not yours to barter with, and now you've put me in a terrible position."

Desmond didn't understand. Yes, the stone was a powerful magical object, but it was only one of the hundreds inside their vault not doing anything. Giving it up to save his father's life had seemed like a no-brainer. This cemented the fact for him that something was terribly wrong.

The real king would never kill someone they owed a favor to. That was more the duke's kind of sabotage.

"I'm sorry to have disappointed you." Desmond lowered his eyes to the floor as he tried to think of his next move.

Rasmus barked harsh laughter. "Then you have a hard way of showing it. How much of my life must I spend cleaning up your messes?"

Just this once, if I recall correctly, was what he wanted to say.

"Then let me clean this one up for you." Desmond placed a hand on his father's shoulder and looked him in the eye. "It wouldn't be right for us to kill someone to whom we owe a favor."

Rasmus' hand came up, gripping the opposite shoulder and squeezing tightly. "I know, and that's why I'm so upset with you. Having to give this order dishonors us, but it must happen for the good of the kingdom."

"Oh yes, Father, I know." Desmond lowered his voice conspiratorially. "I suggest we let one of our oldest enemies do the deed for us instead."

Smiling wide, Rasmus looked over at his son, beaming with pride. "You mean to send them after her?" He licked his lips, knocking his son's arm away and pulling him into a hug. "It's genius. I love it."

Now I have to sell it to the adventurers.

"Of course, I'll send a detachment of men with you." Rasmus winked. "In case we get lucky, and they refuse the quest."

It sounded like a good way to lose a lot of men. "Splendid idea," was what Desmond managed to croak out.

"You go and see to it immediately." The king's red eyes were hard to read. "Don't let me down again."

Desmond bowed. "Your will is my command." He rose, turned, and strode out the door with purpose.

He had to find the adventurers and quickly. They needed to get out of the royal lands as quickly as possible. The thing wearing his father's skin could change its mind at any moment and have the adventurers killed. Now Prince Desmond had to get the group of adventurers to agree to a quest for a reward they should have already received.

No one ever said being a leader was easy.

As soon as he was out of the throne room, he sent a message to Tim. The gist of it was simple. "I'm coming."

CHAPTER TWO

Grant's carriage was big and comfortable, but it wasn't the kind of place a person spent an entire day in.

Waiting in the carriage was kind of like lying in bed all day. After a while, even the soft memory foam hurt Tim's ass. He opened the carriage door and stepped out into the cool night air. If Desmond didn't show up soon, they would probably have to concede the fact he wasn't going to show up. At some point, they'd have to give up and make the long circle around the king's lands back to Promethia.

As it stood, he'd give Desmond until breakfast to make it right.

Stretching his back until it popped, Tim stood straight and looked around. There were still two guards at the gate, but the men had gone back to mostly ignoring them as they waited for new orders. With his stretching done, he felt the familiar urge to pee. What was it with sleeping that made a person run to the bathroom to make water the first thing upon waking?

Wandering off into the woods alone was never a great idea, so he moved to the wall, and once he was out of sight of the guards, he let it rip.

Once he finished peeing the letters of his name on the king's wall, Tim tied up his pants. "Just keeping it classy."

Chuckling, he turned back toward the carriage and saw the others emerging. "What's up, guys?"

Cassie shrugged. "I don't know. ShadowLily said something about a commotion at the gate."

"I think the guards were running around screaming something like pee on the walls." JaKobi snickered. "They were all looking for buckets and rags."

Lorelei stopped about ten feet from the wall. "You can see here where the early-stage pubescent male has left his marking on another man's territory." She pointed and moved her hand like she was tracing something. "As you can see here, there is a pattern."

She turned and looked at Tim. "By God, I think we've solved the case. The markings spell out a name."

"Bitch." Tim coughed into his hand.

"No, that wasn't it." Lorelei smiled demurely. "I'm not impressed because you can write your name on a wall without paint."

Cassie's eyes lit up. "What if I could do it?"

"I'd buy that shit on pay-per-view." Lorelei busted out laughing as soon as she spoke.

They all got a good chuckle out of the joke, but then ShadowLily pointed toward the gate. "Someone is coming. Maybe we should show them the marking and see if they can determine what caused it."

"Got it, don't pee your name on things." Tim winked at her. "Let's find out if this is the prince.

Together they moved to stand by the carriage.

A carriage stopped inside the gate, and Desmond leapt out. The prince tapped his hand against the side of the carriage, and it turned and left. He motioned for the guards to open the gate and walked forward with efficient purpose.

"I'm sorry to have kept you waiting so long. Things in the castle have been rather chaotic since the king woke up." Desmond didn't look very happy about his dad taking a turn for the better.

Cassie got in the prince's face so quickly one of the guards gave a startled shout. "We're not in the business of working with welshers."

"In the most respectful terms, of course." JaKobi eased Cassie back a few steps.

Tim almost sighed in exasperation. They'd gone over this moment a hundred times while they were waiting for the prince to show up. It was plain as day something else was going on, and they'd agreed to give the prince the benefit of the doubt until they heard his side of the story.

This wasn't the plan.

"Would you care to join us for a drink, Desmond? We have one keg left, and it's a long ride back to the inn." Tim motioned toward the carriage.

ShadowLily didn't miss a beat. She strung her arm through Desmond's and led him in the right direction. "We'd be delighted to have you."

One of the guards looked uncertain about letting the prince ride off with people barred from entering the grounds by the king's orders. "Sir?"

Desmond pulled his arm gently out of ShadowLily's and turned to face the man. "It's fine. Go back to your post."

"Yes, sir." The man ran back to the open gate.

Holding out his arm for ShadowLily to take, Desmond smiled. "Tell me more about this beer."

As soon as they were all in the carriage and underway, Cassie turned her frown back on the prince. "Someone's got some explaining to do."

Tim was impressed she wasn't screaming or punching him. The normal Cassie defaulted to solving problems by hitting things hard until they relented or broke. So far, they were marked safe from causing a royal incident, but that could change at any moment.

Turning his attention from Cassie to the prince, Tim took the lead. "I think that's what he's here to do."

Prince Desmond told them everything that had happened since the king woke up from his coma. It was one hell of a story. The king was either under another spell or not the king at all. How something or someone could've replaced him was anyone's guess, but with magic, anything was possible.

"The bastard wanted to kill us," Cassie raged, not concerned for a single second with the bigger picture.

JaKobi was smiling as though he was in the middle of a great fantasy novel and was ready to sink his teeth in. "The king might not be the king?"

"I'm worried the imposter thought Desmond's idea was a good one. If the fake king is on board, it has to be a trap." Lorelei looked at ShadowLily for confirmation.

The mist slayer nodded in confirmation. "Agreed. Before we can help, we need more information."

That's why I love her.

Tim was grinning as he addressed the prince. "Tell us about this quest you want us to take on."

"First things first." Desmond pulled out five pouches of gold. "While I might not be able to secure the stone for you yet, I can and will honor the rest of your quest rewards now."

Everyone accepted their twenty gold as the prince continued. "As for the item, I've sent you a list of what we have available, you merely have to select the item, and it will be messengered to you immediately."

Cassie smiled for the first time since laying eyes on the prince. "It's a start."

Desmond bowed his head. "I promise you this, young

warrior, if completing this next task doesn't free my father, I will steal the stone for you myself."

Cassie saw the sincerity in his eyes as he lifted his head and heard it in his words. "Don't let us down, and we won't let you down."

Desmond bowed his head again in respect. "I swear it."

"That's good enough for me." JaKobi clapped the prince on the back and handed him a mug of beer.

"You're also right." Desmond met each of their eyes in turn. "It's probably a trap."

Tim felt his smile growing as he thought about their previous victories. "Against the odds is kind of what we specialize in."

Desmond nodded. "I'm starting to see that." He waved. "These are the details. You don't have to take on this task, but the fate of the kingdom hangs in the balance."

Quest Received: The Veil of Madness

Something is wrong with the good King Rasmus, and the problem lies hidden within the Veil of Madness. Travel to the location, enter the veil, and stop whatever is happening there. The only additional information I can provide to you is the witch living there is named Cronos. The villagers gave her the title to mock Sonos as she grew older and more powerful in her magical arts.

Since then, she sealed off those lands, and any who enter have been cast out and driven mad by the experience. Now the entire village serves at the whim of Cronos, and she delights in taking her slow revenge. Isadora was her greatest apprentice, and she'll seek vengeance for her death.

Reward: The Stone of Immoratis, even if I have to steal it myself.

Tim gazed around the carriage, seeing what everyone thought of the quest. As far as he could tell, everyone looked on board so he accepted the quest. "We'll find out what's going on, and if something is controlling your father or has replaced him, we'll take care of it."

The relief in Desmond's eyes was palpable. "Thank you." He turned slowly. "All of you. I know I've asked much from you and delivered little, but I will not forget your service to the kingdom."

"You better not," Cassie growled.

They all broke out in laughter.

Desmond was looking at Tim but pointing at Cassie. "I really like this one."

"She grows on you, that's for sure." JaKobi gave her a quick kiss.

Desmond tapped on the roof of the carriage, signaling for it to stop. "The royal seal should be effective for you again, but I ask that you not return until you complete the deed."

The carriage stopped, and Tim opened the door for the prince to exit. "Be safe, Prince Desmond. If all is as you say, your life might also be in danger."

Cassie added, "You can't pay if you're dead."

Nodding, the prince left the carriage. "Do not underestimate Cronos. She is as deadly as she is old."

The door to the carriage closed, and a few moments later they were moving again. Tim fired off a quick message to Grant to let him know they needed to get to the inn, leaned back, and waited for the chaos to ensue.

"The balls on that guy," Cassie stated bluntly.

Lorelei laughed. "Were they spectacular? I didn't even notice."

"Can balls be spectacular?" ShadowLily laughed. "I mostly ignore them."

Tim pretty much did the same thing. "Hey, unless we're going to sing the song, let's get back on track."

"So this is what we know." ShadowLily took over the conversation, not wanting to hear one word about that dreaded song. "If we want a shot at the stone, we have to try and defeat this next dungeon or storm the castle."

Cassie sipped her beer. "You know what I've been saying from the beginning. We need to take that shit."

"I'm willing to give Desmond one more chance, but if he lets us down again…" ShadowLily smirked as she pointed at Cassie. "I'm with her."

Tim raised his hand. "All in favor of giving Desmond one last chance?"

Three more hands shot into the air.

"Then we give him one more shot." He turned to Cassie. "If we end up doing it your way, you call all the shots, and I'll back you one hundred percent."

Cassie looked mollified for the moment. "Fine, but I want dibs on the killing blow."

"Done." Tim was confident he didn't need to check with the others to meet that particular demand.

"Oh, and I don't want to have to tell Eternia that we don't have the stone," Cassie added quickly.

A chorus of "not it" rained across the carriage.

Tim took a fresh beer from JaKobi. "Fine, I'll tell her about our setback, but I want all of you to use this ride to go over your skills and get them updated. We need to make sure we go into the next fight prepared."

"Don't forget to check the auction house for supplemental gear or potions. There are some really good deals, and all you have to do to complete an order is go to Tim's kiosk. He waived the fees for all of us, so use it when you can." ShadowLily *clinked* her glass against his.

Lorelei tapped hers against the two of theirs. "I'll send a message to Roberto and tell him we're coming in hot."

"If I were into dudes, I'd be all over that." JaKobi was clearly thinking about the endless breakfast options that came with marrying a master chef.

Cassie's face turned serious for a moment. "Wait, I'm into dudes. Should I be getting all up on it?"

"How good is the discount on pancakes?" JaKobi mocked as he tried to suppress a laugh.

Cassie dove into his lap. "I think they'd be free but are you willing to give all this up for a few free pancakes?"

"Humm." JaKobi pretended to think about it. "They are really good."

Cassie socked him in the stomach. "And I'm not?"

"Nah, baby, the point is you're so good we'd be rolling in free packers for the rest of our lives." JaKobi held onto her tightly. "Of course I'd never trade you for anything."

"I'm starting to like this free pancake idea. Maybe I could even get Roberto to throw in some breakfast sausage." Cassie laughed at the look of shock on JaKobi's face and nestled back into him.

Tim finished his beer and set the mug down. He hated to be the vibe killer, but they were going to be busy tomorrow, and he wanted to get the grunt work out of the way so he could enjoy their newest dungeon crawl without feeling guilty about not updating his skills.

"Time to focus up. Update your skills, and try to stay quiet until everyone finishes." Tim looked at Cassie.

"Why are you looking at me? I might play a tank on TV, but in real life, I'm a college graduate." Cassie winked. "Me try read book now."

"Finally, someone speaking in a language I can understand." JaKobi beamed from ear to ear.

Tim laughed as he leaned back in his seat to get comfortable.

This was going to take a while.

CHAPTER THREE

Tim watched for a moment as everyone pulled up their interfaces to check their skills.

Normally this part of the process felt a little daunting even though it was incredibly rewarding when he received a tier upgrade, but today it felt like a breath of fresh air. He needed to take his mind off the task in front of them for a bit, and this was the thing to do it.

Doing this next quest for the same reward was rubbing him a bit raw, but the loot they picked up while handling all these side missions was adding up. Everyone in the party had really good gear stacked, and if they kept rocking these boss fights, they would always have top-tier loot. Sometimes it felt good having that shiny thing everyone else was dying to get their hands on.

System Message: You have gained a level.
You have been awarded one skill point.

Tim couldn't help but smile as he started making progress to level forty. Some people hated leveling, but he kind of loved it. It was just like the endgame grind, but instead of gear progression, the player was always chasing the next skill unlock or dungeon they would have access to. For some reason, he couldn't get enough of it.

Like the mouse who only pushed the pleasure button.

He dumped the one stat point in strength, bringing his total to fifteen. The first thing Tim wanted to do was get all his stats to a baseline of twenty. Then he would start stacking Wisdom like he found a pallet of the skill points at a going out of business sale. He sipped his beer and moved onto the first skill update.

Skill Increased: Hex of the Shattered Beast
Rank: Novice three

Good doggy, good doggy. Interesting choice on the manifestation of your beast, but a Golden Retriever can do the job as well as any other breed. To level this skill, you need to keep using it, get creative, and show us you can use it to maximum effect for larger increases.

Tim was already thinking of ways he could use this skill to boost healing. If he didn't heal during Behold My Power and switched to Way of the River right before the hound hit, he might be able to top off everyone's health without having to cast an additional spell. It was never a bad idea to save as much mana as he could so it was there when he needed it. That was one of his highest priorities during fights.

Things started with a bang. Tim hoped they kept going as well with his next update.

Skill Increased: Curse of Sacrifice
Rank: Novice six

No pain, no gain, takes on an entirely new meaning when it's your health stripped away as you deal damage. Still, you used this skill repeatedly, and it's already paying dividends. It won't be long now until you make the apprentice ranks and this skill receives its first perk. Keep up the sacrifice.

Just like with Behold My Power, this curse required him to

pay a price for using it. Having the same thing happen with his previous skill made it so Tim didn't feel the pain anymore. The only thing he had to be careful about was losing too much health attacking and then not dodging quick enough to avoid an attack. At that point, he might as well have been throwing himself off a cliff. The way he used the skill now, his worst-case scenario still left him two or three mistakes away from being dead.

Tim didn't make a lot of mistakes.

Skill Increased: Night Vision
Rank: Apprentice one
It never ceases to amaze us how much time you spend wandering around in the dark. Your eyes are adapting, and at the apprentice ranks, you're more likely to see things in low light conditions. Obtain higher ranks to see when there is no light at all.

Tim used this skill without even thinking about it most of the time. So far he'd noticed that the skill made the light from JaKobi's floating orbs cover more ground. If it was totally dark, he still couldn't make out more than his hand in front of his face, and even then, it was only an outline. If they kept having to fight in caves, this skill would continue leveling all on its own.

He loved having as many passive abilities as possible. It was nice sometimes not to have to think about every minor detail. If he could see, he could see, and if he couldn't, he was leveling the skill. It was the perfect harmony for the player who wanted to do as little work as possible.

Skill Increased: Rectify
Rank: Apprentice four
When the boss wants to make you go splat, but first they wanna supercharge, this is the skill you need to use. You can't remove every boss buff, but the ones you can, will have

a green icon. Use this spell whenever it's off cooldown, and the boss has a buff you need to remove.

Tim loved this skill. The bosses in games were a bunch of tricky bastards and tended to buff up before dealing swathes of big, painful damage. Stopping their ability to do increased damage or shield themselves from it was paramount to their group's success. The line between a boss hitting the enrage timer and winning in time was often down to stopping the boss from buffing up.

Skill Increased: Disturbance
Rank: Apprentice five
Wham, bam, you're dead, but not if you use this skill in time. Bosses will have some interruptible attacks, and it's in your best interest to stop them from happening at any cost. Larger attacks might take more than one interrupt to stop. At the journeyman ranks, this skill receives additional benefits.

He loved nothing more than stopping the boss from doing damage and causing them to fumble their attack and take increased damage for a bit. It didn't happen all the time, but when the boss took that extra damage, it really helped them out. This was a skill he needed to use more. The higher the level, the more it would help his group.

Skill Increased: Quick Feet
Rank: Apprentice Five
Run, run, Rudolph, but try not to choke any more bakers. Yeah, not your finest moment. On the plus side, you used the skill leading to an attack, which you haven't done before. Keep using this skill when you need to move fast, and it will level up quickly.

Hey!

Tim already admitted he wasn't proud of how he acted and made amends with Joaquin. There were all kinds of ways he could justify his actions to himself, but he knew when he'd screwed up even if he didn't like to admit it. The Sisters of Eternal Bliss hung in the back of his mind like a hangover he couldn't shake. He'd get back there one day and find out the truth of what they were doing to the people trapped there.

Skill Increased: Dodge
Rank: Journeyman six
He runs, he jumps, he falls flat on his face. That pretty much sums up your use of this ability. We wish your technique was super cool or clever, but you normally throw your body around like it's a ragdoll and hope for the best. Have a little more respect for yourself.

Tim wanted to argue, but it was true. When he saw trouble coming, he didn't think about *how* to get out of the way. He just did it as quickly as possible. Any damage he took by tossing his body around would be less than what would happen if he ate an attack from the boss. And normally, something Hydration would take care of automatically. Until his last piece of loot, he'd never really had any serious protection and managed to stay alive just fine.

Now he not only looked badass, but he could probably take an extra hit or two before dying. He wasn't exactly sure what direction his class would take him when he started the game, but Tim was ecstatic with where he ended up. This game was so much fun, and they had more crazy fights in front of them to look forward to.

He was ready to find out what was on the other side of the veil of madness and defeat the evil residing there.

Skill Increased: Flame Burst
Rank: Journeyman six
It's kind of amazing how well you use this skill when you don't use it all that often. Come on already. Lighting stuff on fire is cool. Ask your pyrotechnic friend. Continue using Flame Burst, and it'll reward you when you hit the master ranks.

Lighting his enemies on fire was pretty fucking cool, but he also used this skill to keep people away. Sometimes creating a little distance was all he needed to let Cassie take control of the situation. Plus, he could totally make a mountain of s'mores at one time, and not everyone could do that.

Skill Increased: Behold My Power
Rank: Journeyman seven

It's okay to have a pain fetish. Lots of people do. The fact you like to share your pain with your friends is a little unique, but who are we to judge? You're almost at the master ranks with this skill. Keep on hurting your friends and your enemies to level it up.

If they didn't want him hurting his friends, they shouldn't have made the skill so damn appealing. It was one of his favorite skills, and Tim liked to use it to start or end most fights. It was his largest single target damaging ability, and it had saved their ass more than once. They could say what they wanted, but he embraced his class's philosophy on dishing out pain to himself and others to do even more to the boss.

Doing damage to heal was fucking awesome.

Skill Increased: Who Needs a Shield
Rank: Journeyman seven

At least it's not all about hurting your friends. Sometimes you even save them from damage. Who Needs a Shield is your bread and butter for deflecting damage, and you tend to use it at the right times. You've almost reached the master ranks. Get ready for this spell to gain a new perk when you get there.

As if blocking damage and increasing the target's dodge chance wasn't enough. If this skill received an additional benefit, it would be the bee's knees.

Did bees even have knees? Who came up with this shit, anyway?

Tim chuckled as he took another sip of beer. Truth be told he might need a Cleanse, but he would let it ride until they got back to the inn or he finished updating his skills. This wasn't quite the party he expected to be having tonight, but he was doing just fine.

Skill Increased: Divine Light
Rank: Journeyman eight
So now we know why you don't use your Flame Burst as much as you should. You're addicted to shooting light from your fingertips. We get it. It's a cool skill although it can be hard on the mana pool when the fighting gets intense. You use this skill well and are almost at the master ranks. Keep up the good work, and you'll get there shortly.

Tim didn't know why but it felt like the game was being nice to him today. These skill updates were super helpful and encouraging and not exactly what he was used to when he got them. Normally the game was a little more judgmental of his talents. Maybe it was the beer, but it felt like everything was going to work out just fine. In the morning, he'd get to put these new updates to the test.

Skill Increased: Healing Storm
Rank: Journeyman eight
Just like Pacman Jones, you like to make it rain. Okay, so you don't exactly do your thing at the strip club, but imagine how cool it would be if you did. This is your go-to AOE heal, and you know how to use it well. Watch the channeling cost so it doesn't leave you in a pickle.

No kidding.

Tim knew he'd become too reliant on channeling Healing Storm at the end of fights and that needed to change. It wiped out all his mana, and if they were in another situation like their fight with Isadora where zero percent didn't mean the fight was over, it could be trouble. He vowed to make sure when he channeled the spell the next time he did it at the right time, for the right length.

Skill Increased: Cleanse

Rank: Master one
Welcome to the master ranks, again. It must feel good being a master of more than one skill. Cleanse will now automatically cure any debuff at the journeymen ranks and below. With each move you take up the master ranks, your ability to cure master-level debuffs will increase. Right now, you have the base thirty-three percent chance for success.

Cleanse can now also be cast as a group cleanse for an additional mana cost.

Some days it felt like the game was raining down love on him. He knew other people joining the master ranks were probably getting similar benefits to their classes, but this increase felt especially good. Not only did his chance of cleansing master-level spells increase, but the fact he could cast Cleanse on his entire party for an additional cost was huge.

It's going to save me a shit-ton of time.

Tim read over the update again to make sure he understood it. Then he tried to cast the spell. Just like that his buzz was gone.

"What in the fuck, man?" JaKobi poured himself another beer. "Not cool, not fucking cool." He chugged it and poured a second.

ShadowLily laughed. "Let me guess, new spell?"

"She got it in one." Tim touched a finger to his nose. "Sorry, guys, didn't mean to kill your buzz."

JaKobi handed Tim a mug. "Easy enough problem to fix."

Lorelei accepted a fresh drink. "Since we don't have to worry about calories, why not have another."

Tim sipped his new beer and went back to reading his updates.

Skill Increased: Curse of Giving
Rank: Master one
Curse of Giving is becoming one of your favorite spells

to use. It provides periodic damage to the boss and periodic healing to the targets of your stance or stances. The increased damage you received at the journeyman ranks has increased to five percent, and that percentage is now unblockable. At the master ranks, each cast of Curse of Giving places a stack of Shattered World on the target. When the target receives three stacks of Shattered World, the skill will activate and deal a burst of single target damage.

System Message: Achievement Title Granted

This is your third skill to make the master ranks. That's quite an achievement and should be celebrated. You've earned the title "Triple Threat." This title is a display-only achievement and provides no additional benefits.

Did that mean some titles did give bonuses? If so, there was an entire secondary path for gear he'd have to dig into. How to get certain titles with the right benefits would be something they could look into soon. For now, he was excited about the title, and more importantly, the update to Curse of Giving.

Holy shit, that was one hell of an update.

Tim almost spilled his beer as he tried to stand. Then he bumped his head on the roof of the carriage and sat back down, only spilling a small bit. How was a guy supposed to celebrate when he couldn't stand up to dance properly? Asking Grant to pull the carriage over so he could break out the JaKobi shuffle seemed like a crazy idea, so he kept his mouth shut and hoped no one noticed.

"Smooth move." Cassie giggled.

So much for no one noticing.

ShadowLily rubbed his head. "Don't go smashing that pretty little head of yours. I like it the way it is."

Feeling his cheeks turn red but unable to stop it, Tim embraced his mistake. "Sorry, forgot where I was for a second."

"Update was that good, huh?" JaKobi lifted his hand for a high five. "Right on, man!"

Lorelei smiled as if she was indulging children. "You guys mind? I have a few more things to go over."

"Sorry." Tim had a few skills he needed to go over as well.

The last thing he wanted to do was reach the inn and have everyone done with their updates but him. It didn't set a great example when the person in the leadership role didn't get the job done because he was too busy goofing off. Tim set his empty mug to the side and got back to work.

Skill Increased: Healing Orb
Rank: Master three
Splash, splash, splash. Man, you would be a hit at summer pool parties. Not only would you win every water balloon fight without balloons, but you'd heal all the people while doing it. Healing Orb won't receive another major update until you hit the grandmaster ranks, but with each tier increase inside the master ranks, the spell will provide increased healing.

Tim couldn't have thought about a more fitting end to his skill updates. Healing Orb was his oldest skill and his most used talent. Nothing he did kept his group alive more than casting this single spell as many times as possible. If the skill kept getting boosts, he'd make up for some of the power it lost during the update.

Sometimes when things were going right, they turned into a freight train of good luck.

Buffs
Skill Increased: Armor of Eternia
Rank: Journeyman seven
Armor of Eternia will only receive small tier increases until it reaches the master ranks. Don't forget that while your buffs last for eight hours unless specifically stated otherwise, it never hurts to do a buff check before a fight.

That was probably the most considerate reminder he'd ever received in a game. His skill received a slight bump, and he couldn't have been more pleased. It wouldn't be long now until his buffs reached the master ranks and became even more substantial.

Tim couldn't wait.

Skill Increased: Attacks of the Faithful
Rank: Journeyman seven
Like your other buff, this skill will only receive small increases until it reaches the master ranks. That doesn't mean this buff isn't worth its weight in gold. Helping your entire group do more damage is always a winning strategy.

Tim liked to think the easiest way to win a fight was with unrelenting brute force. It wasn't always the best way, and sometimes not everyone made it, but just going ham and trying to destroy the boss as fast as possible got him through more fights than it didn't.

As long as the group could keep up.

The Blue Dagger Society was the best group of gamers he'd ever had the pleasure to game with. None of them were flawless, but they all knew how to excel and didn't make the simple mistakes that would've wiped out many other parties. He loved every single one of them like family and would do anything for them.

Even buy them more beer.

The carriage stopped, and Tim looked over his group. "Drinks are on me tonight. Let's have some fun and take on tomorrow with everything we've got."

"Like we'd ever do anything less." Cassie *clinked* her mug to the others.

ShadowLily opened the door to the carriage. "Let's hurry up and get inside before he makes us do a cheer again."

"Hey, that was fun," Lorelei groused as she followed her out.

Tim motioned for the others to exit. "We'll save the cheer for tomorrow."

"Bro, they need to see our new moves." JaKobi grinned like a madman. "As soon as we take down Cronos, we should bust them out."

"This is going to be epic." Cassie jumped out. "Girls, we're in for a real treat."

Tim looked over at JaKobi with a huge shit-eating grin. "They aren't going to know what hit them."

They climbed out of the carriage and headed for the inn.

CHAPTER FOUR

"I sense a great disturbance…"
In the force, say in the force.
"At the castle," Eternia continued smoothly. "There is a dark cloud hanging there, but it isn't my sister's influence."

Tim hoped for a *Star Wars* line in there, but he wasn't disappointed. In fact, he felt relieved Eternia was confirming Prince Desmond's fears. While it might suck for the kingdom, it meant the prince wasn't dicking them around and could be trusted. The stone was almost in their hands now. One more day and this would all be over.

Turning away from the fireplace, Eternia locked eyes with Tim. "You should be careful when confronting the evil in the castle. There is powerful magic at work. It isn't safe."

"What else can we do?" They both knew there wasn't another way forward except to fight Cronos and whatever was lurking in the castle.

Eternia took the seat by the fireplace in her room and slipped into thought. "Maybe you will find something beyond the veil that will help in the final battle, but even my sight cannot penetrate Cronos' realm."

"So we're in for a real fight then." Tim knew he should've been nervous but pushing into a new dungeon was what he needed right now.

Eternia looked worried enough for the both of them. "Adventurer, it will be the fight of your life."

Tim dropped to one knee. "Thank you for your help."

"You are the one helping me." Eternia motioned for him to rise. "Now go and have fun with your friends. The fight for *The Etheric Coast* continues tomorrow."

He was never one to turn down a good time. "Thank you. Will we see you in the morning?"

"I'll be down to see you off." Eternia flicked her hand, and the door to her room opened.

Tim turned to leave. "Then I'll see you in the morning." The door closed gently behind him as he stepped into the hallway.

He tried to think of something he could do to make a great entrance, but as he started down the stairs, Tim couldn't come up with a single thing he could do that was cooler than Cassie diving off the balcony and through a table. It was one thing when she could do it and not get hurt, but if Tim did it and broke his back, it wouldn't be nearly as funny. So he settled for strolling in and grabbing a beer.

"How did things go with the boss?" JaKobi screwed up his face as if he were expecting bad news.

At least on this front, Tim had nothing but good news. "She understands our difficulties and accepts them."

"I don't accept them. The prince better have something nice for us after all this hassle." Cassie took a swig of her beer.

Lorelei shrugged. "He sure did last time, and you know Cronos is going to drop something epic."

"I could do with a new offhand weapon. I just haven't found anything worthwhile yet." JaKobi looked excited. "Are you sure we can't leave now?"

Gaston strutted into the middle of the bar like he hadn't

ever left. "I'd kind of like to have a beer with my friends before we leave again."

"Stop all that foolish talk this instant," Ernie grumbled as he walked past, heading to his secret rooms at the back of the kitchens. "Goddess or not, I'm too old for this shit."

ShadowLily moved to stand next to her favorite assassin. "Sounds like you guys had one hell of a trip."

"Oh, you know, what happens in Tristholm stays in Tristholm." Gaston accepted a beer from Liz. "Your new friends should be safely back in the desert by now."

"Thank you for getting them home safely." Lorelei hugged Gaston. "I'm going to send Neema a message. See you guys in the morning."

Gaston looked rather put out. "Really? No welcome back party?"

"I promise we'll throw you a huge bash tomorrow, big guy." Tim clapped him on the back. "But we had one hell of a day, and we're going to chillax for a bit."

Gaston took a swig of his beer. "Had a few of those days myself recently. Tomorrow night will be fine, but I expect it to be big. Like, blowing off the doors big."

"Only if we win," Tim replied casually. "Or I should say when we win."

Gaston nodded. "Naturally."

"That guy at the bar with Liz is Grant, our new carriage driver. Be nice." ShadowLily scolded Gaston like a loving older sister as she slipped her arm through Tim's. "I have a quest for you to accomplish upstairs."

Tim felt the grin spreading on his face. "That's my kind of quest." He cast his group Cleanse and let her drag him away.

How people woke up without the fresh scent of coffee in their nostrils always mystified Tim.

Seriously, try it one time, and every day becomes like those old Folgers in your cup commercials. The scent of fresh-brewed coffee gently stimulated the nose and lured the sleepy family members into the kitchen. Somewhere deep inside, he wondered why there wasn't a *Family Guy* parody of that but where Stewie lured them all into the kitchen and killed his family with one of his ray guns. Sure, it might be a little dark, but if the little guy really wanted world domination, he had to start somewhere.

He didn't touch the coffee yet. Instead, he crawled out of bed, surprised to see ShadowLily was still there. After a quick trip to the bathroom, he came back to find ShadowLily enjoying his cup of coffee.

"What?" She shrugged, and the sheet dropped dangerously low. "If you wanted it, you should've taken it with you."

Tim smiled as he headed toward the door. "Trust me when I say those are two smells that should never combine."

The pillow came at him out of nowhere.

"See you downstairs soon," Tim called as he closed the door, chuckling the entire time. "See if she steals my coffee again."

It would be a few minutes before ShadowLily joined him for breakfast. The rest of the group was going to be blown away by how early he was up. It was dangerous to set this new kind of precedent, but when he woke up early, he liked to get up and go with it. As for how Liz always knew when he'd be waking up, he'd never had the courage to ask.

Wait, did she decide when he woke up?

The thought totally blew Tim's mind. She could drop off a cup of coffee at two am, and the smell would wake him before he realized what time it was. Maybe all of this was some kind of sick experiment to make him wake up early. Did ShadowLily put her up to this?

Tim shrugged as he started down the stairs. "At least the coffee's good."

Liz ran around the bar when he appeared. "Good, you got my note."

"What note?" Tim felt a little befuddled. He hadn't had his coffee yet.

"The one on the bottom of your cup, knucklehead." Liz glared at him. "Where is your coffee anyway?"

Tim felt a little embarrassed not to have the steaming cup of joe in his hands after Liz clearly went through some extra trouble this morning. "Um, about that, we might start needing two cups of coffee."

"She's drinking it?" Liz gasped. "Let's hope she doesn't see the note."

For a second there, he thought Liz had been trying to poison him and was upset she poisoned ShadowLily instead, but now he was intrigued about what this note was and why ShadowLily couldn't see it.

Tim reached out and put a comforting hand on Liz's shoulder. "I think you better tell me what's going on."

"Joe's back." She gave a nervous laugh, and her hands flew into the air in exasperation. "Surprise."

Before Tim could respond, Liz continued. "The note was asking you to keep her busy for a bit. Joe wanted to make her something special."

Tim pulled his hand back, held it in front of him, and mimicked pouring into a glass. "If I'm going back up there, I need my cup of coffee."

"Dick!" Liz slapped his arm but went to get his coffee anyway.

With his strength to face the day in hand, Tim ascended the stairs and tried to think of a good distraction. If he wanted to distract her without it being too suspicious, he was going to have to pull out all the stops. He started looking through his inventory until he had on the perfect outfit and equipped it before walking through the door.

Tim had decked himself out in a fully Renaissance look. He was either Sabastian Stann as the Mad Hatter or the infamous Dorian Gray. Whoever he was supposed to be, he looked fucking pimping, and ShadowLily was going to eat him up. She loved all those romancy novels and movies so this was her kind of thing. All he had to do now was set the proper mood.

He walked into the room and dipped his incredibly tall top hat. "Baby, I'm ten-sixths hard for you."

ShadowLily's towel fell to the floor. "Just don't tell my boyfriend, Mr. Hatter. He gets awfully jealous about these things."

"You might as well say that I see what I eat is the same as I eat what I see." Tim unequipped all his clothes and rushed into the arms of the most beautiful woman he'd ever seen.

Liz nudged Tim. "I said buy me some time, not make her late for breakfast."

"What can I say? Things got a little carried away." Tim tried not to laugh at the shocked expression on Liz's face. "Look at the two of them. It all worked out."

Liz topped off his coffee as she watched Joe and ShadowLily chatting. "It sure did."

He felt a bit of sadness coming off her and didn't want to ask what it was about so he pulled her into a side hug. "You'll always have a place here with us. You're part of our family now."

"Thank you." Liz returned the hug, but when she left, there were tears in her eyes.

JaKobi pointed at him. "What was all that about?"

"You know me, always a hit with the ladies." Tim downplayed the situation, mostly because he had no idea what sparked the moment.

If Liz ever needed their help, she would have it in an instant. Tim hoped she knew that whatever it was they were there for her. Maybe he could have ShadowLily or Lorelei find out what was going on and get to the bottom of it. It could be as simple as she needed someone to talk to.

Joe let out a burst of laughter. "No, he didn't."

ShadowLily giggled. "You should see the look on his face when he runs."

Joe slapped his thigh and then looked up at Tim. "Speak of the devil."

"Hey Joe, welcome back." Tim accepted the hearty plate of food and sat.

Joe grinned. "Won't be here for more than a day or two. Just checking in on my girl and Roberto."

"Roberto is the man!" JaKobi decreed.

Cassie was a little more helpful. "We all love him."

"That seems to be the consensus." Joe smiled. "Which is good because I'll be spending more time in Tristholm with Seraphina."

He turned and looked at his daughter. "Just get those portals back up, so I can come to see you more often."

"You know we will." ShadowLily took a bite of her blueberry pancakes. "If you stay another day or two, you could probably avoid the ride back altogether."

Joe looked from her to Tim. "Do you think so?"

"As long as the prince holds up his end of the deal, it's a foregone conclusion." Tim winked at his girl. "ShadowLily could probably handle this one on her own, but we're tagging along to make sure things don't get out of hand."

Cassie slammed her juice down. "Let's fuck this bitch up!"

"Language," Joe chided. "This is a breakfast table, not some bar."

Lorelei grinned. "Actually, it's a breakfast table inside a bar. So swearing is optional but not required."

Joe started laughing. When his belly brushed against the table, the entire thing shook with the depth of his mirth. "Then I'm going to have some more fucking pancakes."

"Not your best work, Dad." ShadowLily poked him with her elbow.

Joe ignored her as he drenched his pancakes in syrup. "What do you expect? I spent the last twenty years not swearing so I could keep you out of the habit. I'm outta practice."

Cassie patted Joe on the leg. "We'll spend an afternoon together sometime, and I'll catch you up to speed with all the new slang."

"I'd be delighted." Joe took a big bite of his blueberry pancakes.

Tim laughed. "Maybe he's not cut out for it. Don't feel any pressure, Joe. You can sit here and not swear too. Some of us like to keep things a little more dignified."

"Damn straight!" JaKobi barked, and the entire table started laughing.

This was what it was all about, saving the world and great times with the people he cared about. He didn't know what would happen today, but he did know there was no one he'd rather experience it with than the Blue Dagger Society.

Eternia missed breakfast, but she met them at the carriage.

"A final word before you leave, adventurers," the goddess called as she walked out onto the covered porch.

Surprising them all, it was Cassie who dropped to one knee first. "Get down, you ungrateful bastards. The goddess is going to give us her blessing."

All of them dropped to a knee in a line, and Eternia moved toward them. She stopped over each adventure touching their heads and saying the words of blessing. When she finished the task, the goddess stepped back and motioned for them to rise.

"Today you face an unknown danger in an unknown land. Take my blessing of protection, and bring home a great victory." Eternia looked as if she were enjoying herself quite a bit.

ShadowLily gave Joe one last hug. "See you soon, Dad."

"Don't do anything crazy." Joe fretted over her.

JaKobi tapped Joe on the shoulder. "Crazy is kind of her specialty."

"I used to like that one." Joe glared at JaKobi's back as he followed Cassie into the carriage.

ShadowLily slapped him playfully on the arm. "You still do." Then she turned and followed the others.

Lorelei pulled Eternia into a hug. "We'll have you back to full strength soon."

"I know you will." The goddess returned the hug warmly and smiled as she watched Lorelei get in the carriage.

Joe pointed at Tim. "You bring my girl home safe."

"I'll do my best."

Joe brushed past him, walking into the inn. "Do better."

Now he sounds like one of my parents.

Turning to face the goddess, Tim couldn't help but smile. "Thank you for seeing us off. We'll return with good news, I promise."

"I see great things in your future adventurer, but first you must conquer the task at hand. Even with my blessing, the victory will be hard-fought." The goddess bent so she could look directly into his eyes. "I believe in you."

Tim's heart almost leapt out of his chest. The goddess believed in them. In their chance for victory. His spirits soared, knowing that the most powerful being in this world was on their side. They could do this. They just had to have a little faith.

Limp Bizkit-style.

"We won't let you down." Tim turned and headed for the carriage.

As he climbed inside, he heard Eternia's voice. "You never do."

This was it. They were about to tackle a brand new dungeon.

He lived for this shit.

CHAPTER FIVE

It was a surprise to find the king in the hidden chambers leading to the family vault.

Since Rasmus awoke from the curse Isadora placed upon him he'd been acting differently. There were times Desmond almost doubted himself when the king acted as he normally would, but then he would miss something simple, and his suspicions would be confirmed all over again.

The secret passages were one of the things the king had seemingly forgotten until now.

Desmond knew his duty, and if this thing wasn't the king, he couldn't let it access the family vault. Their greatest treasures resided within, including the Stone of Immoratis. He'd promised the stone to the adventurers, and he'd be damned if he let the imposter tarnish his reputation again.

Sliding his sword free, Desmond followed the imposter.

It was clear the creature had no idea where it was going, which made following it dangerous. At the same time, he couldn't risk letting the thing get to the vault out of his sight. So Desmond settled for waiting farther back when he saw Rasmus make a mistake. The last thing he wanted was to provoke a confrontation when there might not be a need for one quite yet. It was better to know an enemy completely than to jump into battle without a plan.

The winding, turning, cursing rampage went on for hours until finally, they reached the vault.

The ancient door blocking the way into the royal treasury was made of two things, metal and magic. If he had to guess, Desmond would've said magic played the more significant part. Nothing could open the vault except the blood of a royal, a secret not shared with any due to the possible ramifications.

The last thing they needed was people bumping off the royals to try and break in.

Desmond waited around the corner and watched as the thing tried to open the vault. The key fit in the lock, it even turned, but the door wouldn't open. It had to be incredibly frustrating for the king as he tried to figure out what the problem was.

"The problem is, you're not my father." Desmond gritted his teeth instead of screaming in frustration. Now wasn't the proper time or place to confront the creature.

He slid his sword safely back into his scabbard and watched the king rage as he plotted his next course of action.

The adventurers had deployed to deal with Cronos. Their victory might end all his problems, but it could take days. Longer if they continued dying. They might not have that kind of time before this creature grew impatient and started taking more drastic measures.

The king already threw half the damn castle into the dungeons for some perceived slight or another. Desmond had been sneaking people out for weeks, and the king hardly even noticed. It was almost as if he couldn't tell the difference between one person or another. That or the thing didn't care. The rash actions of the imposter were driving more of the nobles into the open arms of Duke Ravenstorm. It was a nightmare.

If only ending these threats was as easy as waking up.

"Why do you deny me?" King Rasmus slammed his hand against the vault door.

Prince Desmond ducked his head back around the corner as he listened to the thing that was wearing his father's body continue to rage. It was horrible looking into the face he'd loved for so long and seeing someone else. The thought of lifting his sword against his father, even knowing that it wasn't him terrified him. He wasn't sure he would be able to do it unless driven by some desperate need.

What he needed now was the support of the nobles, and he'd never have it with the duke spreading honeyed whispers in their ears. Instead, he'd have to rely on himself and the ones he'd hired to take out Cronos if they could only succeed where all other adventurers had failed.

Then it really would feel like waking up from a bad dream.

"I pray to the goddess to grant strength to the adventurers and let them return to the kingdom quickly," Desmond whispered as he turned away from the king and headed back toward his rooms.

The vault was secure for now, but he had to make sure his mother knew the truth. It took him five minutes to work his way through the maze of corridors before he reached the secret entrance in his chambers. When he exited his room, Prince Desmond's guards fell into step behind him, and he went to see the one person he knew he could still trust.

Mom.

If she didn't know what to do, his mother would at least be able to calm his nerves. While he didn't always listen to her counsel, he always appreciated it. It wasn't often he had someone in his life he could count on to tell him the unvarnished truth. That kind of truth was what he needed right now.

The guards who would normally be waiting outside the king's chambers were gone, and the door was open. Desmond pulled his sword free, letting the steel sing its song of death as he raised the blade high above his head.

Desmond pointed at one of his guards. "Go for backup." He turned to the other. "You're with me."

He moved inside the royal chambers, and that was when he saw the foot. It wasn't like the guard had been knocked unconscious, and his foot was out in the open. Something had ripped the limb off, and the bone was sticking out without a body to be seen. The edges looked gnawed-upon.

"Search the rooms. Look for the king and queen." Desmond knew where the king was, but it wouldn't do him any good to tell his guard what was happening.

The guard grunted his acknowledgment and headed down the corridor to the right. Desmond turned left, making his way toward his mother's room. There was another guard down and two of her servants. He wanted to have hope, but this much death could only mean one thing. He just wasn't ready to believe it yet.

There was a body wedged into the doorframe of his mother's room. Almost as if the woman had been trying to hold the door closed when the top half blew apart. His heart went out to her. It was something truly special when an average person became a hero. Desmond would find out her name and remember it always.

He pushed the door open, and the lower half of the unknown woman's body fell over with a *thud*. The prince stepped around her corpse and entered the room, searching for the thing he most feared to find. His mother's welcoming chamber was empty save for the destruction. People tended to forget that his mother was one hell of a sorceress, and it looked as though she'd brought her entire arsenal to bear. There were holes in the stone where her magic had ripped free large chunks. If the fight lasted much longer, she might've brought the whole damn place down on top of her attacker.

Maybe that was what she was trying to do.

He saw the signs of her magic everywhere as he moved through the space. The attacks grew more frantic, and in her panic, it looked like more of them missed their mark. There was blood on the wall and now on the floor.

If whatever attacked his mother was powerful enough to hurt her, they were in real trouble. Desmond wouldn't be able to kill the king alone, he needed to rally more men to his side, but first, he had to know the truth.

There was only one room left, the queen's bedchamber and entrance to the secret tunnels. The door to the room was gone, along with half of the wall that held it. There was black ichor splattered around the room, but it was nothing compared to the blood. Red felt like it was quickly becoming the only color he could see.

The queen was dead.

Not only was she dead, but she'd been savaged like when the hunting hounds caught a hare. Still, even in death, she left him a message. The door to the secret entrance was open, and there was only one person he'd seen down there for hours. Part of him already felt guilty for not being here, but by the time he saw Rasmus, this horrible deed had already happened.

Desmond wanted to fall at his mother's feet and weep. Instead, he pushed the secret door closed and called for help.

The king ran into the queen's chambers, flanked by several guards. "What happened here?"

Desmond met the king's smiling eyes and looked down at the scorch marks on his robes. "Maybe you should tell me."

The scorch marks disappeared, and the smug expression on Rasmus's face changed to predatory. "The prince has killed the queen. Throw him in the dungeon."

Clutching his sword tight, Desmond prepared to fight.

Then he looked back at his mother's body. Instead of wading into battle, he sheathed his sword and unlatched his sword belt. He tossed the weapon to his guard.

"I'll come peacefully." Desmond turned his eyes back on the king. "You'll never get what you came for."

Rasmus motioned for the guards to take him away. "I guess we'll see."

It was too late to fight back now, and he might have missed his only chance to do so. Striking the king might have forced him to reveal himself, but it would have also given credence to the tale that he killed his mother. Desmond didn't mind others remembering him as a lot of things, but the prince who killed his mother wasn't one he was willing to live with.

The guards shoved him from the room as they left the queen's chambers and headed toward the dungeon.

"Sir, what should I do?" John, his guard asked, clearly wondering if he should try and attack to free the prince.

Desmond stilled his sword hand with a look. "Go tell Brother Khalil what happened and that the kingdom is counting on his friend now more than ever."

"I will do so." John sprinted away as fast as he could.

This wasn't exactly how he'd expected the day to go after his father had awoken. A celebration, a feast, maybe even the announcement of his marriage to a woman he'd never met. The thought of a monster replacing his father and killing his mother never crossed his mind.

The worst part was he might've brought all of this on himself. If the adventurers hadn't killed Isadora, the thing wearing his father's skin might've never woken up. It would've been easier to live with the thought of his father dead than it was to think of himself as alone in the world as he was now. All his hopes rested on the shoulders of five brave adventurers.

It was too late to offer them more help now. He'd have to hope they had what it took to free everyone from this madness.

The bars closed on his cell. Desmond took a seat, feeling the bittersweet sting of injustice. There was only one thing he could do now. He dropped to his knees and prayed.

"Eternia, please shine your strength upon those in need." He looked toward the ceiling of his cell. "If you can carve out a little free time, I wouldn't mind some assistance in whatever form it can be delivered."

CHAPTER SIX

The veil wasn't what Tim expected.

The shimmering surface that separated Cronos's land from the rest of the world looked like a wall formed out of the aurora borealis. Tim had expected something much more sinister than some nice shiny lights. If Cronos was such a monster, why did the borders to her land scream, come right in. We have wonderful and tempting things inside?

It could be a trick, like the Sisters of Eternal Bliss, yet he didn't think it was.

He watched the shining lights ripple across the sky. Behind them, he saw nothing. It was almost as if he were looking into a mirror. Whatever Cronos was hiding beyond the veil, they wouldn't be able to figure it out from this side. They could be walking straight into hell itself and wouldn't be able to tell until they were trapped there.

"I'll give her one thing, Cronos doesn't skimp on the theatrics." Cassie huffed as she looked up into the sky.

JaKobi walked toward the veil and tapped his staff against it. The shimmering wall of light clung to it almost like liquid.

The ember wizard shook off his staff, and the droplets floated back into the veil.

"The real question is, who wants to go first?" JaKobi looked back at Cassie with hopeful eyes.

The tank rushed forward and slung JaKobi over her shoulder. "Why don't we go in together?"

Then they were gone.

"Catch you on the flip." Lorelei ran to catch up.

ShadowLily gave Tim a quick kiss. "We've got this."

"You know it, baby." Tim took one last look at the outside world and stepped through the veil to join his friends.

The sensation of moving through the magic was more like swimming than walking. The veil clung to him in big thick drops, but he could still breathe like normal. It was almost like he stepped inside a lava lamp as the bright colors of the aurora darted past him.

What felt like an eternity passed before he stepped out on the other side. In reality, he'd probably only been inside the veil for ten or twenty seconds, but with the magic pressing in all around it felt longer.

"Holy shit!" Tim breathed as he took in the valley below them and the sky above.

The aurora rose around them like a dome, but it wasn't the flashing lights that caught his eyes. It was the giant wings flapping in the distance. "Is that a dragon?"

JaKobi turned and started walking toward the exit. "Nope. Not going to happen."

"It'll be fine." Tim turned his buddy back toward the dungeon. "Just don't touch his balls."

Lorelei laughed. "Do dragons have balls? You think they'd get in the way with all the flying and the landing."

In his head, he saw a dragon with great big balls trying to land and rolling onto his back to try and protect them with a giant chat bubble over his head saying "ouchie."

"All I'm saying is, I met a guy in the lobby who died trying to figure out the answer to that question. Didn't ask him how successful the attempt was." Tim laughed at the absurdity of it.

"My guess is this one is a lady." ShadowLily grinned. "Maybe even Cronos herself."

JaKobi looked worried. "Why do you have to say stuff like that? You know if you speak it into existence, it can become true."

Cassie laughed. "That's an old wives tale, and lizards don't have balls on the outside. They have them tucked inside like lady parts."

When everyone stared at her, Cassie shrugged. "What, I passed basic biology."

"There goes that dream." Tim was grinning like an idiot. "You know what I think is weird? No one ever talks about dragon shit."

JaKobi laughed. "That's because if it falls on you, there's no one left to talk about it."

"I mean if the things are eating flocks of sheep and entire towns, the poop problem has to be epic." Tim's face took on a serious mien. "I'm sorry we have to raise taxes again. It's just the kingdom cannot keep up with all this dragon shit."

JaKobi grumbled, "Kill the dragons, down with the shit tax!"

"That's how wars get started." Tim finished his little act and turned to see all three women staring at them with their mouths hanging open.

Cassie was the first one to speak. "I can't believe it's me saying this, but focus up, we've got work to do."

"The poop wars, can you imagine?" ShadowLily shook her head at the thought of it. "This is what my entire life is going to be like from now on. I've decided to live with the man who invented poop wars."

Tim kissed her. "You know you love me."

Lorelei laughed and stopped when she realized everyone

was looking at her. "Sorry, I had an image of this happening back in the real world and being on the news."

The spirit archer dropped her voice into a smooth news reporter tone. "Samantha thought today would be like any other day. Then her life changed forever. When poop falls from the sky, tonight at nine."

ShadowLily was laughing but shaking her head at the same time. "You guys are too much."

"I used to be the reserved one." Lorelei snorted. "Guess that ship has sailed."

Cassie pointed into the sky. "Not sure if you noticed, but the dragon is coming back."

The tank was right. The dragon took a wide banking turn and glided straight for them. The monster's feet were the size of cars. Its legs might as well have been school busses. This wasn't only a dragon. It was a giant among dragons.

The megalodragon.

As it landed in front of them, the dragon's claws tore huge chunks out of the land. The trenches were deep enough they'd have to crawl down into them and up the other side if they wanted to continue. The dragon took a few steps forward, shimmered briefly, and a woman in flowing blue robes edged in white replaced it.

"This is my kingdom. You are not welcome here." Cronos looked over the group of adventurers with disdain. "Leave now, and I will spare your lives."

JaKobi elbowed Tim. "See, this is what I was talking about."

Ignoring his friend completely, Tim addressed Cronos. "We've come on behalf of Prince Desmond to end the trouble plaguing the king."

Cronos laughed. "The king suffers a fate of his making. My offer stands unchanged."

Tim didn't know what offer she was speaking about, and he

didn't need to consult the group. They all knew what the stakes were. "Then we refuse."

Cassie stepped to the front of the group. "I'm ready to rumble."

The briefest hint of anger flashed across Cronos' face revealing some hidden rage behind the illusion of serenity. "You've been warned. I will see any further advancement into my realm as hostile, and my forces will attack you on sight. I doubt you'll make it past my defenders, but if you do."

Cronos turned away from them and ran. The ground shook as she changed from a beautiful woman into a terrifying dragon. Fire belched from her mouth as she took to the air, igniting the wet grass and trees before she flew off into the distance.

"Well, that went well." Cassie grinned. "Must not be all that if we're not dead."

Lorelei put an arm around the tank's shoulders. "Or she finds the task beneath her. I mean, look at that."

Even in such a brief visit for Cronos to taunt them, the devastation to the clearing they stood in was immense. Tim didn't want to think what one of those claws would do to him, or the fire for that matter. They couldn't have to face down a dragon to win the dungeon, did they? It didn't seem like a fair test of skill, but he knew if the game put an obstacle in their path, there had to be a way to win.

All they had to do was find it.

"Since they know we're here, Cassie in the front, standard battle formations for everyone else." Tim looked down at the ground. "Until we know there aren't any traps, we take it slow and steady."

There was a path leading through the grass and into the trees of the forest. The logic was simple enough for all of them to follow. Going down the path would lead them to their next fight. There would be time to worry about Cronos if they made it that far. For now, they had to focus on what was right in front of them.

"You got it." Cassie took command. "Stay behind me, and don't get fucking dead."

JaKobi nudged Tim. "That's some award-winning advice right there."

Tim nodded. Staying behind the tank was gaming one-oh-one. If you didn't want to go splat, there were certain rules to follow. While merciless devs could break all rules, they tended not to break that big one unless it led to a devastating mechanic.

He took his spot at the back of the group. This was it. They were finally on their way.

CHAPTER SEVEN

The clear shimmering dome of the boss area was right in front of them.

Cronos' realm was different from the way they normally fought bosses. Most of the time, they could see inside the area and were given a small advantage in the terrain before the fight started. This time they couldn't see a thing. It was like they were looking into a mirror, and Tim didn't like it one bit.

Cassie looked over her shoulder. "Buff and ready check."

"It's like we're pros." Tim couldn't help but smile.

There was a point when a person started gaming with people long enough they didn't check their companions' buffs anymore. They assumed they were in place. Even then, after a close win, some of the best gamers would make a statement like, "We did that without the crit buff." Everyone cringed at first. Then they realize they beat a boss while missing out on a five percent bonus the entire time.

Thus making them completely badass.

When they first entered the game, Tim was always the one calling these minor things out, but now Cassie was taking over, and he loved it. So he didn't have to look at his user interface to check, Tim cast all three of his buffs. He felt the other players' buffs increasing his stats as well.

"Follow Cassie. I'll try and call out the changes as they come." Tim looked at everyone. "If you see something weird, say something."

Cassie walked into the shimmering mist. "Don't fuck this up. Mama wants to leave this dungeon with a new pair of dragon skin shoes."

"That's cold." JaKobi gave Tim a high five and went through the barrier.

Tim followed the ember wizard through the mist and ended up standing in a clearing much like Isadora's. The ground wasn't littered with scorch marks so they had that going for them, but there was blood on the closely shaved grass.

Was that shit?

"I thought we were kidding about the dragon shit." Tim looked at the rather large pile of droppings and knew they were too small to have come from the dragon.

Lorelei kicked a pile with the toe of her boot. "It's probably a bear."

"Bear?" ShadowLily looked worried, like she was having a *The Revenant* flashback. "Are you sure?"

Lorelei bent and looked at a couple of different piles. "I guess it could be a werebear or something mixed with a bear, but yeah, for the most part, I'm pretty sure."

She stood with the expression on her face saying she was about to wreck their day. "There's also more than one."

"This is going to be interesting." Cassie started moving forward. "Might as well find out what we're in for."

Tim kept his head moving from side to side, but there was nowhere a giant-ass bear could be hiding, let alone two. There was a pillar of rocks to their left, but while they could hide behind it in ones and twos, it wasn't big enough to hide a bear unless it was a cub.

A man walked into the clearing wearing simple overalls with a wide-brimmed hat. The man had the look of a farmer. If it wasn't for the two bear cubs at his side, that's exactly what he would have been. Maybe it was more like he was a breeder. A quick look at his official title said bear farmer, whatever that meant.

"Mistress said you'd be coming." He spat on the ground. "Ain't normally old Eli's place to be getting involved with the killing. I'm a farmer by nature, but Mistress says do a thing, and it's best get done before she comes back to check on it."

The two small grizzly cubs rubbed against his legs like cats. "Now it ain't my place to be offering you a deal, but walk away from this. It'd be in your best interest. You seem like good folks. I'd hate for you to die."

Tim appreciated the deal, but they couldn't walk away. No matter what Eli thought of Cronos he was pretty sure she was as evil as they came. It was like someone saying they grew organic when really they were out there spraying their GMO with pesticides. Most of the time, when things sounded too good to be true, they were a scam. Whatever Cronos offered wouldn't change what she'd done to the king.

Good people didn't fight dirty.

"We'd love to take you up on the offer, but first, you'd have to tell us what she did to the king and how to fix it." If Cronos guaranteed the real king or the death of the imposter, maybe they could work something out.

Eli pulled a Bermuda grass seed head from the tip of his cap and started chewing on the end. "All that's above old Eli's pay grade. If you're spoiling for a fight, then it's a fight you'll have."

The bear farmer stepped back and easily doubled in size. The two small scythes the boss held appeared to be all the weaponry Eli needed, as long as you included the giant bear trap strapped to his back. Tim wasn't sure that counted as a weapon, but it could be deadly in the right situations.

Tim had no idea what direction this fight was going to go in, but for now, he decided to be happy he had three targets to cast Curse of Giving on instead of one.

"I can't wait to try bear for the first time." Cassie charged into battle with a scream that shook the ground.

Tim immediately noticed that his curse on the bears wasn't doing any damage but didn't know what he could do about it. Eli and the bears weren't showing any buffs he could remove, and his curse was ticking away on the boss himself. This was going to be a long fight if they couldn't kill the bears. He wasn't crazy about Cassie taking all the extra damage.

"The bears aren't taking damage. Focus on Eli!" Tim shouted as he fired a blast of Curse of Sacrifice and followed it up with a quick Healing Orb on himself to spread Hydration to anyone that had taken damage.

Cassie seemed to have things in hand so it gave him time to look around. Maybe now that the fight had started, there would be some clue about what they had to do to harm the bears. It was amazing what details the devs would slip in as a fight progressed. As for now, he wasn't picking up anything new, but that didn't mean it wouldn't happen soon.

Tim normally hated fights where the bosses had pets that players couldn't kill. In those situations, the players usually had to deal with an additional mechanic from the pet. On the plus side, in those fights, the pets didn't do a lot of additional damage, and all they had to do was beat the mechanic and kill the boss. It didn't get much easier than that.

Unless there was a twist.

ShadowLily was having a hell of a time trying to dart in and out of the two bears and the boss while doing damage. So far she'd managed to be nearly flawless, but it was a risky game that she couldn't win forever. She might have to take a back seat on the DPS until they figured out what mechanics the boss had in store for them.

The words to Behold My Power tumbled from his lips effortlessly, like he'd said them a million times before. As the first shockwave of damage tore through his group, Eli met his eye and smiled. For the first time in a fight, Tim had the feeling he fucked up, and it was going to cost them.

Eli grunted when Cassie hit him, but he wasn't taking damage anymore. With each blow of her staff, he grew slightly larger, and the bears took on a red hue. Tim was pretty sure he'd figured out the game. If they hit Eli when he wasn't supposed to be taking damage, he got a little bit bigger, and the bears got a little bit more enraged. If they hit the bears at the wrong time, they would also get bigger, and Eli would get enraged.

It was a hell of a tightrope to have to walk.

Paying attention in this fight was going to be a huge deal. Their entire success or failure depended on how quickly they could manage the switches. By casting Behold My Power before knowing what the fight's mechanics were, he was putting them in a hole. When his spell hit, the bears were going to get a huge enrage boost, and Eli might grow a foot.

How had he been so wrong about the mechanics early on?

At least the mistake was early enough in the fight they would recover, but Tim had to warn the others. "No long-lasting spells. If we miss a change, it's going to suck."

Behold My Power hit and didn't do a damn thing to Cassie's health, but Eli grew a little bit larger, and the bears were doing slightly more damage. They were still in Phase One so everything was manageable, but they sure weren't making things easy on themselves.

"You were saying!" Cassie let out an evil laugh as she redirected an attack from one of the bears into Eli.

Eli was taking damage again. There wasn't time for fancy talking. The changes came too quickly. There was only one thing that would get them on track fast enough. He had to make the calls.

"Switch!" Tim watched as everyone followed Cassie's lead and started damaging Eli again.

The boss was down ten percent in health, and the bears were slightly behind him. When they switched damage back to Eli, the animals he controlled stayed enraged and larger than when the fight started. So the effects of their missed attacks were cumulative for the entire fight.

This was going to be rough.

Tim knew that he couldn't stop some of his attacks from having their DOTs linger on the boss, but then he noticed during the next switch that all of the DOTs only ticked once then faded away. It meant they could use spells with DOTs, but they would risk either the boss or the bears taking one tick of damage if they didn't time the switch right. He wasn't going to tell the others what to do yet, but for now, Curse of Giving was off the table.

Tim needed to stick with the pure healing of Healing Orb and Curse of Sacrifice for now. He wasn't willing to keep putting stacks on the enemy only to make them stronger. Divine Light would also work to boost healing and DPS, but only if he timed it right. The spell did his most single-target damage, and landing a hit at the wrong time wouldn't help their cause any more than casting DOTs would.

"Switch!" Tim cried as Eli took a zero percent fireball to the head.

The bears were still small enough they were taking a good amount of damage per attack. The real question he had to face now was, did they have to kill the bears simultaneously to avoid a larger enrage or could they pick them off one at a time?

"Focus on one of the bears until it gets to ten percent, then switch to the other." It'd be a waste of time if they didn't need to kill them at the same time, but if they did, it was the only way they had a chance.

"Switch!" All their damage went back to Eli.

Tim blasted the bear farmer with Divine Light and Curse of Sacrifice on repeat until he needed to use Healing Orb. Then he kicked himself. Early in the fight, he should've used his Hex Beast instead of Behold My Power, but he couldn't do it now. Not until the next switch.

Eli hit eighty percent health and sent out a blast wave that dropped them all to fifty percent health instantly. Thankfully his Healing Storm didn't cause any damage, and Tim could use it as long as his mana was in a good place. Before he could cast the big heal, he had to cast three quick Healing Orbs to get Hydration on everyone. Then he put his hands in the air and called down Eternia's healing rain.

Their health was back in a good place and climbing rapidly. Tim cut off the costly spell and let the HOTs finish carrying them to full health. So far, nothing too crazy happened, and the fight was going well. There were a few nicks to heal with ShadowLily, but Lorelei and JaKobi had gone relatively untouched until the boss' special attack at eighty percent.

ShadowLily had a look of frustration on her face that melee characters get when the boss is always moving around, and getting the proper positioning sucks ass. It was hard not to get hit with four claws, two scythes, and two sets of big-ass bear jaws all striking simultaneously. It was a wonder they hadn't gutted Cassie yet, but the tank was redirecting blows and dancing from side to side to keep them guessing.

Watching the tank do her thing was impressive. He'd never have the courage to stand close and eat all that damage. Getting hit in *The Etheric Coast* still hurt. Getting ripped apart by bear claws might not have the same sting it did in the real world, but she was feeling every damn hit. Tim had never been more impressed with their tank's fortitude than he was now.

Not that Cassie's constant movement made things any easier for ShadowLily. The mist slayer had to sync her attacks to Cassie's rhythm, and it was throwing her off. While she was frustrated, he was happy she wasn't going YOLO and taking a bunch of damage just to get her numbers back up.

The first bear hit ten percent health, and they all switched over to the next target without being told. In some groups switching off the target they wanted to be kept alive would have felt like a minor miracle, but not with Blue Dagger Society. They managed to burn another five percent before the animal stopped taking damage and they needed to switch back to the boss.

"Switch!" Tim called as he sent Curse of Sacrifice straight at Eli.

A blast of pure sunlight rocketed past him and through one of the bears before striking Eli. The bear's health didn't move, but the red tint around Eli grew a fraction darker.

"Shit, sorry guys!" JaKobi called as he blasted Eli again, this time making sure not to hit the cub.

The attack dropped the boss' health to seventy-five percent, and he let out a roar of rage. With a single motion, he swept them back to the far side of the clearing. Tim tried to move, but he was stuck in place while Eli used one of his scythes to cut the palm of each hand before placing them on top of the bear's heads.

The bear at ninety percent health snarled and growled as it stripped his health away, while the bear at five percent looked content as its health bar started to fill back up. When the boss stopped his cast, one bear was sitting at fifty percent and the other at forty-five.

They needed a new plan.

If Eli could equalize the bears' health, then two things were probably true. They needed to kill the bears simultaneously to avoid an enrage mechanic, and it didn't matter if they split the damage as long as they didn't kill one of them. He was trying to think of a plan when Eli called to them.

"Nothing I hate worse than vermin that won't take a hint." The bear farmer pulled the giant trap from his back and set it on the ground. Then he wound it up like a set of clacking teeth and let it go.

Tim couldn't believe Eli's big move was one wind-up bear trap. Seriously, they wouldn't even have to try and avoid it. This was like asking an NFL running back to dodge a parked car. When something was that easy, it had to be a trap.

"Get ready for it," Tim called.

The twinkle returned to Eli's eyes as he clapped his hands. Then the one trap turned into ten, then a hundred. They were clacking toward them in waves, but there were gaps in the pattern. All they had to do was move into the empty spots without getting hit.

Tim was pretty sure each of them could survive being hit by a single trap. One wasn't a problem. The real issue was they were coming in waves, so if they couldn't get the person out in time, they'd keep getting hit by them until they looked like the victim in one of the *Saw* films.

The only person that their group needed to worry about was JaKobi. Tim was pretty sure he could handle this, but he wasn't going to fare too much better than his fireball-hurling buddy. Everyone else in their party might as well have been a ninja-like dodge master. It was too late to get the entire benefit now, but if this attack came again later, it would be the perfect time for Who Needs a Shield. The extra dodge percentage would give the ember wizard a fighting chance.

"Son of a—" JaKobi let out a startled cry as Cassie used her chain to yank him toward her.

She pulled JaKobi onto her back and dodged the next set of traps with ease. "Don't you worry about a thing, baby. I've got you."

It was awkward seeing the five-foot-nothing girl giving a piggyback ride to the six-foot-tall man. His chest towered over her shoulders, leaving his arms free to cast spells if he needed to.

"Good morning, Vietnam!" JaKobi cried in his best Robin Williams voice as he started blasting fireballs toward the boss.

The fire stopped two feet short of the boss, and ash washed over the three of them like a cool autumn breeze. "Totally unfair."

"Only person who should be saying that is me." Cassie dumped JaKobi on his ass as the last of the traps went clacking past them.

Eli stepped forward with his hand scythes at the ready. "What are you waiting for?"

"Just seeing if that ugly corn-fed mug of yours was up for round two." Cassie swirled her bō staff around her like a tornado.

"Attack!" Eli sent the bears running toward them, his eyes gleaming with malicious purpose.

Tim had a sinking feeling in his chest just like the seconds after casting Behold My Power in the first phase of the fight. "Check who's taking damage before going wild!"

As he finished screaming the order, he saw a fireball launch into the sky.

"Couldn't be sure," JaKobi called as he waited to see if the bears took damage from the tank before attacking again.

Lorelei fired an arrow, just nicking one of the bears. "It's Eli!"

Cassie picked up the bears as the rest of the group transferred their attacks to the boss. They had to make a push here. The internal clock in Tim's head was screaming that the fight was taking too fucking long and if they didn't speed things up, they would get stomped at the end. Two enraged bears and a boss would be a huge problem. One he didn't think they would survive for more than a few seconds.

"When he switches back, try to kill one of those bears." Tim knew they would be pushing their luck, but the healing was light, and their DPS was pretty on point to make a big push.

Lorelei tried to be the voice of reason. "Eli isn't even at fifty percent yet."

Cassie laughed out loud. "I can't believe I'm the one saying this, but we should wait."

"Come on, where's your sense of adventure? Tim called. "Let's get a little reckless."

JaKobi blasted Eli with his Phoenix. "Uh oh, my man Tim's got one of his crazy plans, and I'm totally on board."

"Is it the 'we're all going to die' kind?" ShadowLily mocked as she rolled in front of the boss and slashed him three times before fading behind him and landing a critical backstab.

Tim laughed. "Only one way to find out."

"Switch!"

As one, the entire group pivoted to the bear on Eli's right with forty-five percent health. With every single one of them focused on the bear, it went down quickly. Thirty percent, Tim cast three Healing Orb. Twenty percent, he cast Curse of Giving on the other bear. Ten percent seemed like the right time to drop Who Needs a Shield.

The bear on the right died, and the remaining bear instantly turned into a full-sized grizzly. There was a bright red shine to it, and Tim knew it was fully enraged. He looked over at the creature knowing this next part was going to hurt. The buffs on the bear said it was doing three hundred percent increased damage, and they were about to switch into a phase where they couldn't even hurt the damn thing, let alone kill it.

Maybe this wasn't the best plan he ever had.

"Switch!" Tim screamed like he was a Roman general. "I want this bear fucker hurting!"

He felt some of the tension lift as the group laughed at him as much as what he said. Tim hit Eli with Curse of Giving. He figured that if he hit him right at the beginning of a switch, then the timing would be about spot on or close enough that he was willing to risk it. His DPS during the fight wasn't going to be an issue. The real problem was going to be keeping Cassie alive.

There were a few seconds left before he could activate his plan. If he did it too soon, they'd miss the switch, and Eli would also get a huge boost in DPS. If he acted too late, they wouldn't get the big chunk of the bear they needed to take it out. He fell into a rhythm of casting Curse of Sacrifice on repeat until he executed the next phase of his new plan.

Tim cast Hex of the Shattered Beast on Cassie. He never considered that the beast might attack Eli when this was over because he was the boss. He'd hoped that it would go after the thing doing the most damage, which right now was the enraged grizzly.

Cassie was taking so much damage it was all he could do to keep up with it. Tim made a mental note that if he wanted to try this fight again, they needed to wait at least one more phase before hitting the crazy and killing one of the bears early as he asked them to do this time. That was a move they should've only pulled when they out-geared the dungeon and not during their first attempt at the fight.

"Switch," Tim screamed as his beast started to move.

The red-blurring Golden Retriever slammed into the bear and burst out the other side in a sea of red mist. Even being enraged and taking less damage than usual the single attack stripped away half of its health. The beam of pure sunlight that hit it next cut that number in half again. Five seconds later and the enraged grizzly hit the ground as dead as its twin.

Eli waved his hand again, sending them back to the beginning opposite side of the clearing as he started pacing back and forth. "You monsters killed my babies!"

Eli kept screaming the words at them. Each time he did, the boss grew in size. The small farmer was now over twelve feet tall, and his skin was tinged a pinkish color. "Those bears were my fucking family!"

Instead of bear traps, Eli started spinning in a circle, and hand scythes flew out from him in intervals. Tim tried casting Disturbance out of desperation, but it didn't stop the attack. There was still a pattern to the scythes, but they came on twice as fast as the bear traps had, and all of them were getting nicked. When they came out of this phase, the only thing that mattered was burning the boss down until he lay dead at their feet.

They wouldn't make it through another round, especially if Eli kept getting stronger now that the bears were dead.

"I want you to light this guy up like the Fourth of July. Every attack, every buff, anything you have, we need it now." Tim sent out a small burst of Healing Storm and a round of Healing Orb.

Eli didn't wait for his scythes to stop flying before he charged at Cassie. Tim's world turned into pure madness, but he shut out all the distractions and focused on what mattered. The healing. It was nice that he had a single-target spell for damage that didn't cost a boatload of mana. He could cast Curse of Sacrifice almost all day, as long as he didn't let it zap too much of his health before topping himself off.

The boss hit fifteen percent health, but there wasn't a switch to save him this time. The group continued hammering away, and the bear farmer didn't have a chance. ShadowLily rolled in front of the boss and leapt up, jabbing both of her daggers deep into Eli's stomach. She ripped them out wide, splattering herself in gore. As Eli fell to the side, clutching the horrible wound, he gave one final gurgle before the rest of the group finished him off with ease.

The body disappeared in a beautiful swirl of golden motes, and the blood on ShadowLily slowly did the same. It was crazy to watch the red drops lift into the air and burst into golden globes of light before drifting to the heavens.

ShadowLily let out a battle cry. "We did it!"

All of them raised their weapons into their air and screamed!

Let Cronos hear their cries and learn of their victory. They were coming for her.

CHAPTER EIGHT

"That was something else." Cassie looked at Tim. "Have you ever seen anything like that?"

Tim shook his head. "You mean bear traps acting like The Joker's teeth? I've never seen anything like that in a game."

"Dude, that was awesome." JaKobi pumped his fist, looking at the chest longingly before turning to look at his girlfriend. "Except for when you had to carry me."

Cassie kissed him. "If the choice is between you getting killed and me carrying you, you better climb aboard."

"I plan on doing that later." JaKobi winked.

Lorelei moved toward the chest. "If I can't get laid, I'm getting loot first."

No one objected.

Tim was looking forward to returning to the desert, if for nothing else so Lorelei could spend some time with Neema. Their spirit archer deserved to be happy, and right now, she was the only one having to struggle without their significant other around. It was funny how he never really liked being in a relationship until it was with the right one. Then he couldn't imagine his life without her.

"Bow of the Slaughtered Bear." Lorelei turned, firing a series of arrows across the clearing to test the new weapon. "Adds a DOT and increased endurance."

The old bow disappeared off her back, and the new one replaced it. "Normally, I'd pass, but the base damage is so much higher, it doesn't matter what the other stats are."

Tim had found a few items like that in games. Sometimes it was on purpose, and sometimes his new favorite weapon got hit with the nerf hammer. Nothing sucked worse than logging into the game he loved and seeing his stats reduced drastically. Thankfully that hadn't happened in *The Etheric Coast*, and he hoped it never would.

Instead of going to the chest, Tim hugged Lorelei. "We'll be back in the desert soon."

"Ain't had nothing 'twixt these nethers that don't run on hand power in a good long while." Lorelei looked dead serious.

JaKobi was grinning. "I could stand to hear more."

Cassie slapped him in the chest. "You forgot Mal's part."

"No, I didn't. I just wanted to hear more." JaKobi snickered.

Tim felt the oomph when Cassie hit the wizard in the stomach. "Don't you ruin my *Firefly* with your lecherous ways."

"I'll lech if I want to." JaKobi laughed and pulled the feisty tank into his arms. "Just maybe out of earshot." He rubbed his stomach and winced.

A quick Healing Orb took care of the worst of JaKobi's damage. "I thought it was kinda funny."

"I was impressed you got Lorelei to watch it with you." ShadowLily looked around at the group. "What? She doesn't strike me as a science fiction kind of girl."

Lorelei laughed. "I wasn't until these two snuck me into a video session. Kind of breaks the game immersion, but the show was worth it."

He'd never even thought about trying to stream outside content inside the game. Things seemed too chaotic for something as simple as watching movies. Plus, he kind of liked stepping out of the real world for a bit. Sure, he missed watching his old favorites, but when he wanted entertainment, all he had to do was go downstairs and find Gaston. The assassin was always up to something.

"*Firefly* is awesome. Of that, there is no doubt." Tim motioned to the chest. "Ladies first."

Cassie tapped him on the chest as she passed. "This is what being a gentleman looks like, JaKobi. Take notes."

"I brought chocolate." JaKobi held up a small bar wrapped in waxed paper.

Cassie snatched the chocolate out of his hands. "I take it back. You're doing just fine."

ShadowLily nudged Tim. "What, no chocolate for me?"

"Nope, just that good loving," Tim replied, cool as a cucumber.

Laughing, the mist slayer moved toward the chest. "I think I'll settle for what's behind door number two."

"Sick burn!" JaKobi doubled over with laughter.

Tim clutched his back, looking wounded. "Et tu, JaKobi. Et tu."

Ignoring the two men, ShadowLily placed her hand on the chest and turned, looking excited. "Hat of the Dubious Farmer."

ShadowLily equipped the hat, but with her leather armor, she looked more like Anne Bonny than a farmer. "Increased dexterity, and dodge. Plus, I kind of like how it looks."

"That's because it's hot." Tim liked a woman who didn't take shit from anyone, and no one represented that like his favorite female pirate.

Cassie ran toward the chest. "Let's hope three is still the luckiest number."

The tank placed her hand on the chest. "Leather Pants of the Dancing Bears." She equipped the new pants and smiled wider than a kid at summer camp getting their first delivery from home. "Increases bonuses to all my new skills, and a huge boost to dexterity."

"Man, this loot is all awesome." JaKobi walked toward the chest. "Book of Burning Shadows."

He cast a fireball watching the trail of flames it left in its wake. "Seriously makes my fireball leave a trail that does damage to anything it hits. I love this game."

Tim's excitement built as he laid his hand on the chest. He felt a small surge of power, and the familiar message appeared.

Item Received: Bearhide Wrist Guards of the Faithful

Dalton Red was a priest in the western woods. For a time, he lost himself in nature and lived among the bears. When he returned from the wild, he was a changed man, a healer who damaged the guilty to heal the needy. Eventually, the villagers drove him off, but his memory lives on in these wrist guards through those who wear them.

+1 Endurance +1 Wisdom

Special Ability: The Bear Necessities

If you take damage that would've normally killed you, you will reset to one hit point. The price of this miraculous ability is the low, low cost of seventy percent of your remaining party members' hit points.

Not exactly the piece of gear he was expecting, but the special ability was ridiculous. It was almost like a resurrection spell. The only difference was that not only would he need to be able to heal himself immediately, but everyone in Tim's group would need a huge amount of heals to get back in the fight. One wrong move while any of that was going on, and they were all dead.

Still, the wrist guards would give them a chance when everything else failed.

"Guys, you're not going to believe this." Tim gave them the lowdown on his new item.

JaKobi gave him a wicked high five. "That's fucking

awesome, bro!"

"Let's see if you're saying that after he zaps you to thirty percent health." Cassie laughed, but her expression turned serious as she looked at Tim. "If you think that gadget of yours is going to activate, try and give me a little warning so I can pop a cooldown."

Tim nodded. If there was time, he would give her all the warning he could.

"Are you guys ready to move out?" Tim looked around at the group, wondering if anyone needed to take a break.

No one said anything, and Cassie moved to the front of the pack. "Follow me, but I don't think you're going to like it."

"What do you mean?" Tim looked around the clearing and the path leading to their next destination and didn't see anything amiss.

"You have to look up." Cassie pointed into the distance.

Lorelei blinked a few times and whispered, "Is that a fucking castle?"

"Of course Cronos would have a floating castle." Shadow-Lily's eyes narrowed. "I doubt she's flying supplies up there on her back so there has to be another way in."

Tim looked up at the castle and at the expectant faces of his group. "My guess is we'll find the way up at the end of this path."

"And another boss to go with it." Cassie was grinning as she thought about the chance for more loot.

"All right, Cassie, lead the way." The tank turned and led them into the forest, and Tim followed.

If Eternia told him he'd be fighting in a castle in the sky by the end of the day, Tim would've called her a nutter. Maybe not to her face, mind you, but he would've thought it. Castles in the sky felt like endgame stuff, not the kind of thing you took on while climbing the ranks. Still, it was beautiful, and Tim was happy Cassie pointed it out to him.

The group started walking, and he knew that this was their day. Nothing would stop them now.

"Whoa," JaKobi said with wonder in his voice.

Tim felt the same way. They were closer to the castle in the sky now, and while it was magnificent, it was the magical lift in the town below that claimed their attention. A disk the size of a city block rose into the air carrying carts and people to move the supplies. Then after twenty minutes, it descended again, right into the shimmering mist of the boss dome covering the building.

"At least we know right where the boss is." Cassie sounded ready to rumble.

Tim looked down in the valley and couldn't disagree, but it was the long trip down and through the town that had him worried. With no trash mobs between the entrance and the first boss, this might be the only place they would run into some unless the castle was full of them. His best guess was still that they wouldn't reach the boss without fighting something else first.

Moving down the switchbacks into the valley didn't trigger a fight or a boulder chasing them, so things were going relatively well so far. The pine trees faded, and orchards of citrus and fruit replaced them. The farmland was empty, which seemed odd in the middle of the day unless they expected trouble or were luring them into a trap.

"It's a little too quiet." Lorelei had her bow out as she scanned the horizon for threats.

JaKobi bounced a small ball of flames between his hands. "It's like that moment in horror or action movies right before all hell breaks loose."

"Thanks for calming my nerves." ShadowLily gave the

wizard a dirty look before dropping into stealth.

Tim tried to ease the tension. "What you can't see is her putting a sign on your back that says, eat the wizard first."

When no one laughed, he continued. "Come on guys, when have we ever been stopped by a little trash? It's not like Cronos is going to appear and slaughter us."

"I hate it when he's right." Cassie picked up the pace.

On the outskirts of town, they saw their first two people. The men were huge, and their arms looked like the kind of things Mr. Olympia would be jealous about. When Tim noticed the giant axes slung over their backs, he realized why their arms were so big. The axes weren't Paul Bunyon big, but they were larger than anything he'd seen at the hardware store by far.

"Those ax heads have to be three feet long." Cassie whistled. "Let's hope they only know how to use them to fell trees."

Tim nudged her forward. "I'm dying to find out."

Cassie moved forward and whistled to get the lumberjacks' attention. "How many fucks, does a woodchuck fuck, when a woodchuck chucks fucks."

"Say it again, sister!" JaKobi let loose with a massive fireball.

Tim cast Curse of Giving on both of the lumberjacks and couldn't stop from smiling. Sure, she replaced some of the chucks with fucks, but for some reason, he was cracking up. He wondered what the lumberjacks must be thinking. Both of them might be questioning if it was okay for them to cut someone in half who was clearly mentally challenged.

Cassie answered that question for them when her staff brushed aside their wild swings with ease and conked them on their heads. Fire washed over them, and arrows started to appear in their arms as if they ran into a rabid porcupine.

Curse of Sacrifice wiped out most of the damage Cassie had taken so far, and the lumberjacks were already under fifty percent health.

ShadowLily appeared behind one of the targets, slamming her daggers into the lumberjack's back before rolling under a swing aimed at Cassie and making the same attack from the front. When the lumberjack staggered forward, she slit his throat and danced away.

One of them was down. Now it was mop-up duty.

Seeing the other man fall enraged the remaining lumberjack and he started swinging his ax in wide arcs, forcing them to retreat. His skin was pulsing red, and Tim felt lucky that his health was only at fifteen percent.

Cassie and the remaining lumberjack clashed, and despite her new class, she was staggered by the increased damage. It was everything Tim could do to keep her alive as the rest of the group finished off the target.

"You were saying something about trash being easy?" Cassie looked at the two dead lumberjacks as their bodies turned into golden swirls of light.

Tim nodded. It was a fair assessment of the fight. "Looks like we shouldn't kill them when their health is too far apart."

"You think?" ShadowLily quipped.

"Yeah, I'll watch out for that next time." Cassie laced her words with sarcasm that would have made Denis Leary proud.

I just want coffee-flavored coffee.

They lived so everything was fine, and they figured out that the health thing might be a recurring mechanic in some of the upcoming fights. All they had to do was learn from the first couple of trash packs, then clean them up in a rinse and repeat fashion. These fights weren't there to stress them out but to teach them mechanics and give them a little coin since the bosses mostly just dropped loot.

All they had to do now was keep their wits about them, and they'd make it to the boss without an issue.

The next group was two lumberjacks and a man with brass knuckles. "Remember, try not to kill any of them until they're all under ten percent. Then we should try and AOE them down."

Cassie pointed at Tim. "Get that shield thing ready."

He wanted to cast his Hex Beast, but it was too unpredictable in this scenario. If the beast took out one of the men early and two of them enraged, they would be in trouble. Instead, he had Who Needs a Shield tucked away in the back of his mind if things turned sour.

Three Curse of Giving casts were enough to keep Cassie at full health, letting him have the option of using other skills for fun. Curse of Sacrifice and Divine Light were his skills of choice for the moment, and doing lots of damage was the name of the game as Tim used his tracks to try and balance out the enemies' health. At around fifteen percent health ShadowLily blinked out of existence, and Tim knew one of the men would die in the next five seconds.

"Blast 'em." Tim started channeling Flame Burst at all three targets like he was the pyrotechnics director at a monster truck rally.

JaKobi hesitated. "I thought you said ten percent?"

"Just go," Tim yelled as ShadowLily appeared and started her attack.

"Oh shit!" The ember wizard caught on to what was about to happen and fired his Sunbeam.

Lorelei was moving forward with a dexterity that would have made Legolas jealous as she pounded arrows into the last target.

Just like that, the fight was over.

"That went much better." Cassie grinned. "I didn't feel a thing."

Lorelei pointed in the distance. "How do you feel about a little five on five?"

"Not as good as I felt about three on five," Cassie grumbled.

It turned out five wasn't much harder than three as long as

Cassie could keep control of all five of them herself. If one of them got away, it turned the fight into a bit of a mess. Thankfully with five Curse of Giving casts on her, Tim had plenty of time to use Snare or do straight DPS to even out the enemies' health.

They moved through the town picking off groups of two, three, and five until they reached the building housing the magical lift and the boss. He'd almost expected the doors to open and for ten men to stream out as the final battle before the boss fight, but nothing as exciting as that occurred. They stood in an empty square facing the building. There was nothing left for them to do but open the door and get to work.

"Buff up bitches." Cassie cast her buffs on the group.

Tim reapplied his buffs to the party and moved into his spot behind the tank. "Lead the way."

Cassie smashed her staff against the giant wooden doors. "Open Sesame."

The doors swung open, and she turned to look at the group. "That's never worked before."

"I don't think it was the words." Tim pointed past Cassie to a man standing in the center of the circular room.

He was beckoning them to step inside.

Cassie looked back at Tim. "I have a bad feeling about this."

"That's my line." Tim winked at her. "Let's go kick that little guy's ass."

JaKobi leaned in. "They said that when I had Oddjob and Proximity mines, it didn't work out well for the big guys."

"Encouragement, you big oaf." ShadowLily elbowed the wizard in the ribs like Cassie would have.

JaKobi rubbed the injury smiling. "What? It's not like my girl ever loses a fight."

"Damn right, I don't." Cassie stepped into the building. "Hey Shorty, I got something for you."

The boss' laughter filled their ears.

CHAPTER NINE

"Please come inside." The gatekeeper beckoned.

The boss stood before them, all of five feet tall as he hunched with age. His walking staff was more of a cane the way he clung to it with quiet desperation, and yet he beckoned them inside with open arms.

Cassie led the way, moving slowly and looking for traps, but Tim doubted she would find any. This was their next boss fight, and while the gatekeeper might not look like much now, that didn't have to last forever. Or he'd have help as the farmer did with the bears. Whatever was going to happen, Tim knew they weren't going to be facing down a little old man. Heroes didn't go around kicking the crap out of senior citizens.

"I just need to see your token, and we'll get you straight up to Mistress Cronos." The gatekeeper held out his hand.

Cassie looked back at Tim and mouthed, "Token?" When he gave a slight shake of the head, she addressed the boss. "Think of us as uninvited guests."

"Oh, that simply won't do." The gatekeeper snapped his fingers, and the doors to the lift closed, sealing them all inside the room.

He pulled a pair of reading glasses from inside his robes. "Cronos only accepts *invited* guests. As for the uninvited?" He motioned behind himself. "I have help."

Two men walked out from hidden rooms on either side of the gatekeeper. The fuckers were gigantic. If the members of their group were midsized compacts, these two brutes were Greyhound buses. They made Shaq look like he was an itty-bitty little guy, and anyone who played *Shaq Fu* knew that wasn't the case.

Tim would've called them monsters, but they were giant humans with biceps the size of semi-truck cabs. Before the doors closed, Tim spotted huge cranks in each room. The gatekeeper's helpers must've lifted the platform by cranking it like Arnold at the beginning of Conan when his captor forced him to spin the wheel of pain.

There wasn't a lift?

Magic was a real trip sometimes. His mind started wondering if the cranks were necessary or if whatever moved the platform up to the castle was illusioned so they couldn't see it. If the cranks were only for show, the two men could be highly trained fighters. At this point, he wouldn't put anything past Cronos.

"Normally, I'd offer the ill-informed a chance to leave, but the bear farmer was my friend." The gatekeeper's eyes glowed red for a moment. "I am not adjusting to the news of his passing well."

The older man snapped his fingers again. He lifted into the air on a small disk of pure magic, where he hovered over the shoulders of the two giant guards. Sledgehammers with heads the size of a small SUV appeared next to the men, and they lifted them with practiced efficiency.

"Don't go splat," Tim whispered to Cassie.

The shadow dancer turned to glare at him. "I'm the one who makes them go splat."

"She said it." JaKobi chuckled.

Cassie let out a growl of frustration and charged into battle. "Just be happy these aren't your nuts." She swung her bō staff in a wicked arc right at one of the giants' loin cloth-covered undercarriages.

Tim winced even though the giant wasn't on his side.

The first giant went down in a heap, exhaling a great breath as he tried to control the pain. If there was one thing every man universally appreciated, it was how much taking a hit right to the boys hurt. Sure, it was also good for a chuckle, but deep down, they were all thinking of a time it happened to them.

"Now that's just rude." The gatekeeper sent a blast of energy from his staff at the tank.

Cassie rolled out of the way, and the fight started in earnest. Blasts of magical energy from the gatekeeper's staff kept the tank off-balance enough that the second guard had time to recover. Tim pulled up his interface and almost expected it to say Master Blaster, but instead, the hulking twins were Dee and Dum. It was just their luck that they had to face two huge guys named after the creepiest things from his childhood.

If he never had to think of the Walrus and the Carpenter again, it would be too soon.

Tim shook off the shock of their names and got to work casting three Curse of Giving. He was happy to see that all three targets were taking damage, so they weren't going into another fight that would force them to switch targets constantly. That was fun for a battle or two, but having to work between multiple targets for an entire dungeon could get tedious. His guess was there was a shared health pool here, and they needed to time things right or face the consequences.

"Don't kill any of them until we see if their health balances out or if they have some other trick up their sleeve." Tim cast

Hex of the Shattered Beast on Cassie as the hammers started to fall.

The real trick here would be trying not to kill one of them too early. If they let two of the three get enraged even for a moment, it would mean they fucked up and were about to take a trip to see their caseworkers. Of course, that strictly depended on if he was guessing the mechanics of the fight correctly. So far he was making a lot of assumptions based on the trash they faced on the way into the boss fight without any kind of concrete evidence to back them up.

Cassie and ShadowLily had their hands full dodging the two massive hammers and blasts of energy from the cackling gatekeeper as he whizzed about on his disk of magic. Tim tried to think of which one they should take out first, but he didn't have an answer yet. The damage seemed to be coming in pretty even increments so he wasn't feeling overwhelmed on the healing front.

Waiting for confirmation he was on the right track was killing him.

Tim's Shattered Beast ran across the room, leaving a red streak in its wake. Before hitting the boss, it split into three, and each target took the damage it had done to Cassie. The spell was freaking awesome, and he hadn't nearly given the developers the praise they deserved. The spell was more versatile than he'd given it credit for, and he needed to use it every time it was off cooldown.

Feeling like the momentum was on their side, Tim cast Behold My Power on Dee because he was the brute with the highest health and blasted Dum with Curse of Sacrifice to top off Cassie's health.

So far the fight was going well, but that normally meant things were about to change. Tim kept casting heals as he watched the three enemies' health plummet. The three of them were taking pretty even damage, but they weren't making any real progress yet. Maybe what they needed to do was focus all their energy on a single target,

"Everyone focus on Dee," Tim called as he switched his attacks over to the same target.

JaKobi fired one last fireball at Dum before switching. "What? I didn't want the big guy to feel left out."

Dee's health was at seventy percent, while the other two were hovering around eighty-five. With the group's full attention focused on one target, the hit points started flying off the sledgehammer-wielding guard in huge chunks. Sixty percent flew by, but when they hit fifty percent, a wall of energy slammed into them, and they all began to take periodic damage.

Tim tried to cast Cleanse, but nothing happened.

The gatekeeper continued to cackle as the trio pushed the adventurers back to the entrance, and the two guards moved to stand under his hovering disk. With a wave of his staff, the gatekeeper cast a spell, and Dee's health rose.

Tim almost cried out in anger, but he realized the other two members' health was dropping. This was the best-case scenario for them because they could figure out which of the targets took the most damage and focus on them until the health reset. Then they could rinse and repeat until the fight was over.

As long as there weren't any other big wrinkles.

The floor started to spin in a slow counterclockwise motion. *That's a new twist.* The real question was if the entire room was turning or only the outside walls as a way to disorient them. Overall it was an odd effect. His best guess was that they were spinning, and the walls were static. What was happening in the room didn't matter. All they had to do was focus on the task at hand and kill the damn boss.

Red lines appeared on the floor, and Tim moved until he was standing outside them. Apparently, what was happening in the room did matter. The lines on the floor started pulsing with magical energy and flames erupted from the crevices. When the blasts of magical fire receded, the floor was whole again, and they could move without being worried about being damaged.

Until the effect happened again.

Tim made sure Healing Orb blanketed the group. "Watch your feet for the fire, and let's see what kind of damage Dum takes this time."

"If he gets to ten percent, switch to something else." Cassie ran back toward the bosses. "The last thing we can afford to do is kill one of these guys early."

At that moment, he felt like Cassie was channeling his energy, and Tim felt a sense of pride knowing they were on the same page.

The second phase of the fight went much like the first except for the occasional fissures of fire that erupted at their feet. The healing was more intense due to the constant movement slowing down his casting. The flames erupting from the floor didn't help with the movement problems, and whenever anyone tried to eke out a little too much DPS, it cost them. He wanted to scream, keep moving, but getting burned tended to serve as its own best reminder not to slow down.

In short, the battle with the gatekeeper was a chaotic mess, and Tim loved it. Dodge, heal, damage, heal, it was all a blur as he kept his feet moving and his party alive. He wasn't even watching the bosses' health bars anymore unless it was a quick check to make sure he wasn't going to kill one of them.

After all his fussing, he wasn't going to be the one to screw this up.

Dum hit twenty-five percent health, and a wave of energy and the DOT that came with it hit them. Every third pulse, the DOT hit them with a double-tap of damage. The healing wasn't the worst he'd ever had to deal with, but it stopped him from being able to recharge his mana the way he wanted to during the downtime. The bosses' health equalized again, and now all three were sitting at sixty percent.

"What do you think, time to pick on the little guy?" Tim kept casting as he watched the gatekeeper zip around.

"Let's do it." JaKobi's eyes were tracking the gatekeeper as he wove around in the air.

ShadowLily huffed. "I'll stay on Dum."

Tim hadn't thought about her not being able to target the gatekeeper in the air effectively. It was a good plan though, albeit unintentional. If they could get two of the three's health down to ten percent, they might be able to push for the win during the next phase. All they had to do was survive this one first.

It was going to be a wild ride, but they were ready for it.

Along with the fissures on the floor that spat fire, now there was a beam of light that shot from the center of the room to a fixed point on one of the outer walls. As the room spun, they had to jump over the ankle-high beam as they passed it. Tim didn't want to find out if the magical beam did damage or was only a stun. Either way, it would be bad. Getting stunned into a sledgehammer or having a firepit open beneath them would make for a bad day.

"Watch your feet." Tim made the call as second nature as breathing.

He doubted the group needed another reminder, but it was his job to say the right things to keep their focus sharp. So after the call, he didn't check to see what the others were doing. He did what he did best and kept healing.

Cassie used her chain to try and pull the boss down closer for ShadowLily to get a hit in, but the gatekeeper wiggled out of her grasp before he was in the mist slayer's range. Not perturbed for a second, she kept working on Dee, as the others used the distraction to do some serious damage to the little old guy. The gatekeeper's health was nearing fifteen percent.

"Remember, don't kill him. Switch to Dee or Dum when he's at ten." Tim leapt over the beam, and threw himself to the side to avoid a burst of fire from the floor, then rolled into a crouch laughing maniacally. He could dodge attacks with the best of them.

Holy shit, were his pants on fire?

Tim quickly stood and doused the flame with a Healing Orb before sending another two orbs flying into the scrum. Now that everyone had the Hydrate buff, he returned his attention to the bosses and reapplied Curse of Giving to each of them. Cassie's health looked perfect, and everyone else's was ticking up nicely as Hydrate did its thing. He almost ate another set of flames as he cast Divine Light on the gatekeeper but got lucky.

It was time to tighten things up.

"I've had about enough of that!" the gatekeeper roared. Bolts of magical energy flew out of the bottom of his disk, striking all of them.

Right when things had been going so well.

Tim cast Who Needs a Shield, hoping that Hydrate and the heals from his three curses would be enough to lift Cassie's health back to full while he dealt with the rest of their party. A fresh round of Healing Orb and a burst of Healing Storm got their health looking good, but his mana was in the shitter. Big time.

Time to use those special abilities.

With his mana regeneration doubled for the moment, Tim tried not to cast a single spell to get the full benefit of the regeneration. With all the healing over time spells he had going, everyone's health could handle a few seconds of inattention as he scanned the room for any sign of what would come next.

The gatekeeper's health was at thirteen percent, and Dum was at fifty percent. Dee had gone mostly untouched during this phase and was sitting at fifty-nine percent health. There was no way they were getting out of this phase with a chance to win in the next one unless they sped things up. With the gatekeeper's DOT doing more damage during each stage and Tim's mana taking the hits from the additional ground AOE damage, they weren't going to last forever.

If they couldn't find a way to pick up the pace, they would face an enrage, and he hated the idea of dying that way worse than if they made a simple mistake. Things were getting intense, but so far, it felt like they were still in control.

With his mana bolstered, Tim got back to work by topping off Cassie's health. Then he focused his energy on Dum. The only way this would work was if they got at least two of them so low that pulling the extra health from Dee didn't matter. Sixty percent health only went so far when spread between three people.

The gatekeeper hit ten percent health, and Dum was at twenty when the phase changed. Once again, they were swept to the back of the room and hit with the DOT effect. This time every second and third pulse had a double-tap of damage. The damage over time effect was a real pain in his ass. It continually stopped him from being able to recharge his mana while the others were getting a breather. It would have been nice if the attack was interruptible, but it looked like it was one of those things built into the fight they would have to keep dealing with.

If they made it to a fourth phase, He'd try to use his interrupt anyway. Otherwise, he'd save it for the nasty AOE from the bottom of the gatekeeper's disk. That particular attack was devastating and would probably happen quickly during this phase because of the boss' lower health.

Dee screamed as his health ripped away before stabilizing at twenty-five percent. Dum's health was almost the same at twentyish percent, while the gatekeeper managed to pull a little more from the twins and was sitting at thirty percent health.

They'd done a number on the trio during the last phase, but did they have enough to bring it home now?

Tim had a distinct feeling that this was it. If they didn't win during this phase, the bosses might enrage anyway. Facing three enraged bosses at sub-five percent didn't seem like a good way to win. If they didn't kill them all before the phase change, they would have to drop at least one of them and hope for the best. The risk was doing it soon enough and potentially facing all three bosses versus only the two. If they were flawless, maybe they could kill two of them first.

It was a lot to process.

Now there was also a beam coming at them below shoulder height. So while they were trying to kill the boss, they would be jumping over one beam, ducking under another, and avoiding fire that shot up from the floor like the infamous fire swamps of the *Princess Bride*. It was going to be chaotic, but they had this if they stayed calm.

Tim called his final instructions. "Keep your wits about you. I want the gatekeeper under ten. Then we kill Dum."

"That's not very nice!" Dum roared and charged.

Holy shit, they can hear us.

Cassie intercepted the giant with the sledgehammer before it could hit him. Then his world devolved into a series of small tasks. Heal. Jump. Heal. Duck. Heal. *Oh shit, my pants are on fire.*

Despite all the craziness of the fight swirling around him, Tim found his calm center and focused on his job. He couldn't worry about what the other members of his group were doing. His only task was keeping them alive. His mana pool was as dry as the Mojave desert, but he had enough juice left to see them through this if they went a little faster.

The gatekeeper flew above them, ready to release his shower of magical sparks, and Tim screamed, "Interrupt the boss!"

Almost as one, the entire group shifted and blasted the boss.

It was a frivolous call for him to make when every second of DPS counted, and he had no idea if it would work, but it was worth the risk. If they ate another round of damage that dropped the entire party under fifty percent health, they wouldn't be around to finish the fight.

Instead of the sparks, the gatekeeper's disk surrounded him with energy like a shield. The interrupts worked to stop the attack, and his health was now at eight percent. Dee was at twenty-five percent, and the edges of his hammer were pulsing with red light. Dum's hammer was pulsing as well, but his health was at fifteen percent.

Was this their moment?

Tim thought the pulses on the hammer might mean the phase was about to change so they had to push it now, or else they'd be facing three enraged bosses with over ten percent health.

He sucked in a deep breath and made the call. "Get me a couple of DOTs on the gatekeeper and kill Dum!"

The gatekeeper's health dipped as Tim reapplied Curse of Giving. His hope was the DOTs would shave off another percentage or two while they dealt with Dum. Jump, roll, duck, dodge—finally he blasted him with Curse of Sacrifice. Dum's health was taking a relentless beating. The giant tried to fight them off, but he didn't have the strength to stop their relentless assault.

When Dum died, ShadowLily and Cassie switched their attacks to Dee while the rest of them focused on the gatekeeper. With five percent health left the boss didn't stand much of a chance, but they'd almost tapped out their resources. A beam of sun and a cluster of glowing arrows did most of the work. What the gatekeeper hated was Tim's Divine Light.

The gatekeeper went down in a cry of anguish.

Dee let out a roar of rage and swept his hammer across the room, sending them all back to the entrance with ten percent health. The phase changed, but without the gatekeeper to summon any new magic, the floor and the beams stayed the same. What didn't stay the same was Dee. He doubled in size, and the top of his sledgehammer sprouted spikes like a bat from a zombie flick.

Ten percent was a better number than Tim hoped for when it took them so long to defeat the first of the three. That said, a full ten percent seemed like a big ask from his crew when Dee was fully enraged, and they were running on fumes. At least there hadn't been a DOT to worry about with the gatekeeper being dead, so he was getting a little breather before making the final big push.

An invisible barrier held back Dee, but the hate in his eyes promised nothing but pain as soon as he was released.

Tim pulled Cassie into a quick hug. "Just live."

"I plan on it." The tank kept her eyes on Tim's for a moment. "You know what they say about giants, right?"

She let out a little giggle as she turned her attention back to Dee. "Little cocks."

Dee let out a growl that shattered the barrier, and the fight was on.

Cassie rushed to meet the enraged boss head-on as the rest of them got to work doing whatever DPS they could manage.

The first thing Tim did was cast Hex of the Shattered Beast. The one thing he was certain of was that the boss would do a shit ton of damage. If he could send some of that back his way, even better. After that, his only concern was keeping Cassie alive. He reapplied Curse of Giving, cast Healing Orb, and put Curse of Sacrifice on repeat as he fell into a rhythm.

Run, dodge, curse.

Cassie was getting hammered despite blowing all her cooldowns, but the boss was at three percent health. Tim's Hex Beast activated. His favorite Golden Retriever slammed into the boss, bursting out of his back in a shower of red mist. Dee's health dropped by a full two percent as ShadowLily rolled in front of him. The mist slayer slammed her daggers into his stomach three times before rolling back behind the boss and repeating the attack until he was dead.

Dee fell to the floor, and Tim stared at his corpse as the beam of light that was about to cut him in half disappeared. He was so involved in the fight that the fact they won took a few moments to settle over him. Then he screamed in pure joy.

They'd done it. The gatekeeper was dead.

CHAPTER TEN

Cassie sat in the middle of the room. "I'm going to need a gym membership."

"Tell me about it. I can barely move." JaKobi flopped down next to her.

Tim blasted the entire group with a Cleanse and topped off their health. It completely refreshed his weary muscles, but his brain was still in fight mode. They'd won the battle, but it had been a close thing.

If they had to go back through the dungeon, even with the power of foresight, he wasn't sure they could've handled the fight any differently. The reality was that even knowing the boss's moves, the fights could've easily gone either way.

One of the tricky things about leveling was the players never got a chance to balance their gear before moving to the next challenge.

In fact, for most of the leveling process, players were normally in a mismatch of crappy gear and goofy colors. *The Etheric Coast* had one up on most other titles when it came to gear because the drops came so frequently it always felt like they were moving forward. It sure didn't hurt that all their drops were character and class-specific, either. The group was always getting rewarded with what felt like quality loot. Tim couldn't count the number of MMOs he'd played where he hit max level and didn't have a single piece of gear that he didn't want to toss in the trash instantly.

That was when the real struggle started, the loot grind.

Normally players were forced to progress through a series of events to get the best gear—solo and small group content, followed by dungeons, followed by raids of increasing difficulty. There was a gear progression at each level. Raids got the best loot, but the least of it. Then the next raid came out, and the loot was a little better, and yes, sometimes there was even a story associated with the new instance. Not that the loot-hungry minions noticed.

Who cared about a good story when there were shinies and world firsts to claim?

Tim always kind of liked the story element in raids, but it was hard to watch cutscenes when some guy was in your headphones screaming about how cool his dick looked wrapped in purple cellophane. He didn't know what it was with gamers, but the odder the character, the better the player. Not always, but he'd seen it enough to say it was more than a trend. Still, when a gamer wanted to listen to a cinematic about how to save the princess from the evil baddie, the last image they wanted floating through their mind was a big purple dick.

Like a summer sausage gone wrong.

Tim shook his head, clearing out the images of bad gaming experiences, and took a moment to thank Eternia for his new friends. Without them being inside *The Etheric Coast* with him, the game wouldn't be nearly as enjoyable. It was true when they said what made gaming special was the people. Reaching down, Tim pulled Cassie and JaKobi back to their feet.

"Cassie, dodger of hammers, I think you should go first." Tim pointed at the golden chest. "Show us the way."

The tank walked toward the treasure chest with a good deal of swagger. "Don't mind if I do."

ShadowLily appeared next to Tim. "You know I had to dodge those hammers too."

"Let her have this. It's her favorite thing," Tim whispered back. "Don't think for one second I wouldn't always pick you for my team first."

"Don't you forget it." ShadowLily poked him in the ribs as the tank laid her hand on the chest.

Cassie turned, the glow on her face radiating elation. "Hammer Staff of the Reckless."

The tank equipped her new staff and swung it around. A small sledgehammer head capped each end of the two-inch-thick shaft. It was the kind of thing she could use to put a dent in a big set of heavy armor.

"It feels different, but the bonuses are awesome." Cassie motioned toward the chest. "Come on, who's next?"

It didn't look like anyone wanted to go next after such a great roll. Say one thing about gamers. They were a superstitious bunch. Like everyone knew the football player who wore the same socks all season, gamers had all kinds of weird rituals. Take a sip of Code Red, a bong rip, and a bite of pizza was his best friend Xander's favorite pre-fight ritual. Tim normally closed his eyes for a second and hit his newest music mix so the perfect tunes played in the background while he kicked ass.

He moved toward the chest and rested his hand on the top.

Item received: That's not a Brown Spot Leather Pants

What in the fuck was that? His new pants better not have a big gross brown spot over the ass because some healer a long time ago shit himself during an intense fight. Tim wasn't a coward. He was proud to say that his bowels stayed intact every single time he got smashed into itty-bitty bits.

Ivan wasn't the best healer, and he was an even worse soldier, but he did one thing well. Ivan could run as if the

devil herself was chasing him. The man could dodge and roll away from trouble with the best of them. Their problem was Ivan was always running in the wrong direction. It got to the point where if they needed something done, they'd teleport Ivan to the front, knowing he'd be back in a minute. While the healer never actually shit himself, he earned the name brown spot because he always ran away from trouble.

+3 Endurance +2 Dexterity +4 Intelligence +3 Wisdom
Special Ability: Flee
Whenever you're running away from danger, you'll receive a five percent bonus to speed.

Whoa.

Those pants were pretty freaking awesome. Yeah, Tim didn't like the idea of being associated with a coward, but he did like the special ability and the stats. If he was honest with himself, there were a lot of times he had to run away during fights.

Sometimes he activated Quick Feet, but other times he was running because he didn't want to get trampled. The extra dexterity and Flee ability should make surviving a little easier, even at the roughest of times.

"Leather pants, with a bonus to running away." Tim left out the name of the pants on purpose.

Lorelei let out a very unladylike giggle that ended in a couple of snorts. "Running away, huh? Okay, Mr. Brown Spot."

He was never going to live this down.

"Why don't you go next? Maybe you can pick up a pair of yellow crotch panties of the ruthless." Tim wasn't bitter, not one bit.

Lorelei smiled at him but wagged her finger. "I swear to Eternia if there is something yellow in here, I'm going to shoot you."

"Not if I run away." Tim laughed with her.

Placing her hand on the chest, Lorelei let out a squeal of glee and turned. "Leather Gloves of the Spirit Archer. Bonuses to everything I care about and a special ability to add ten percent critical hit chance to my next attack."

"Gimme some of that." JaKobi looked at the gloves with envy.

ShadowLily pushed the wizard forward. "Be my guest."

"Don't mind if I do." The robe hid his strut, but they all knew he was walking as proudly as Cassie had.

JaKobi put his hand on the chest, turned, and an instant later did a fist pump that would've made Tiger Woods jealous.

"Necklace of the Ember God." A solid gold chain set with a ruby at the center appeared around JaKobi's neck. "You don't even want to know." The wizard's eyes said he was dying for someone to ask him about it.

Tim felt his curiosity bubbling and couldn't stop himself. "Spill the beans."

"Lets me double-cast a single spell, once per fight." JaKobi brushed off his shoulder. "Shit's about to get real."

It was an amazing skill. Tim thought about the damage and healing he could do with a double cast of Behold My Power. Using the special ability at the right time would be a big bonus for their group. There was no doubt in his mind that the ember wizard would figure out the right time to use the skill and exploit it to its full potential.

"Man, I only get to run away from stuff." Tim might have sounded disappointed, but he was thankful his new pants didn't have a brown spot.

Lorelei shrugged. "It's still useful, especially the way you play."

"Tell me about it." ShadowLily laughed. "For a guy who hates running, you sure do a lot of it."

The mist slayer walked toward the chest and settled her hand on it. She looked smugly satisfied when she turned to face the group. "Earrings of Critical Slaughter. Boosts to all the right stats, but the special ability is the kicker."

Pulling her daggers free, ShadowLily launched into a series of complex-looking attacks. "After three critical hits, the next critical hit receives an additional twenty-five percent damage boost. It's a persistent skill, so it's active all the time."

"That's huge!" Tim ran to her and pulled her into a hug. "You're going to destroy Cronos."

Cassie coughed. "*We're* going to destroy that dragon bitch."

"Damn right we are," Lorelei and JaKobi said in unison and stared at each other.

Tim laughed. "It's entirely possible we're spending way too much time together."

The chest burst into beautiful golden motes and drifted toward the heavens as the doors to the gatehouse opened into the castle's courtyard.

"Looks like we won't have to look for a way up." Cassie moved toward the door, and the rest of the group followed.

"It doesn't feel like we're floating in the air." Lorelei looked over the edge.

JaKobi was standing at the edge of the castle grounds peeing into the air and watching as it fell hundreds of feet below them to splatter on the rooftops. "It sure is a long way down."

Laughter burst from Tim's mouth before he could contain it. He knew he started all of this by peeing his name on the king's wall like a little boy in the snow, but he still couldn't resist throwing a dig at his friend. "Way to keep it classy."

JaKobi dropped his robes back in place before turning to face the group. "I don't like having magic used on me without my consent."

"Consent is key." Cassie slammed her elbow into his gut. "But next time you have to take a leak, try and do it with a little more style."

ShadowLily was squatting by the edge. "I could try, but I'm not sure I could get it over the edge."

Lorelei slapped her forehead. "You guys are too much."

"Just making sure my bud doesn't feel awkward being himself, even if it means peeing off the side of the castle on the poor little town folks." ShadowLily winked.

Tim was about to break out in the JaKobi shuffle when he saw a lady walking toward them. "Cassie, eyes front."

"It's not Cronos." The tank dropped into her fighting stance anyway.

JaKobi moved into position, flames rippling across his hands. "Nope, it's Trashnos."

It was Tim's turn to be exasperated. "Let's not make calling the trash Trashnos a thing." Dropping his voice so only Cassie could hear. "He's probably right, and this is our first battle."

Cassie laughed. "Let's call them Trashions. It's self-explanatory."

"Or we could call them trash like normal." Tim dropped into his stance. "Put on your game face. It's time to roll."

The woman wore all-white fabric with the edges dyed a deep purple color. "Mistress Cronos isn't accepting visitors."

"She's expecting us." Cassie flashed a feral grin. "Although I'm surprised she's too scared to show herself."

Deep rich laughter rumbled from the woman in white's belly. "Cronos isn't scared of anyone. She merely deems your presence not worthy of her attention."

Cassie snorted. "Tell that to the gatekeeper and bear farmer."

"No reason to rub her face in it," Tim chided. "It's gotta be hard being staked out like the sacrificial goat."

JaKobi motioned toward the woman. "The way behind us is clear. You can leave whenever you like."

The purple jewel set at the top of the woman's staff pulsed along with the matching jewel on her necklace. "The time for talk is over."

A blast of pure magical energy ripped from the jewel at the top of the staff. It sprayed all of them with its power. The DOT hit hard, and Tim got to work fixing the damage as Cassie charged into the fight.

Instead of dropping into his traditional stance, Tim used Way of the River instead. Now the damage he dealt would be returned to the entire group as healing. He started with his usual Curse of Giving and cast Hex of the Shattered Beast on Cassie. Then it was up to his single-target damage and healing abilities to carry the day. Curse of Sacrifice and Healing Orb would be what he needed to ensure the outcome ended in their favor.

Cassie didn't seem too worried about the magical damage. Her protection against that particular type of damage must've been a lot stronger than his. The single blast they'd taken at the beginning of the fight hurt a lot more than he expected, and it had him starting to think about boosting his resistances.

Now that Cassie had control of the woman, he wouldn't have to be worried about taking damage unless the Trashion used the AOE again.

The purple mage's health was going down at a decent clip, but she put up more of a fight than the previous trash they faced. When Shattered Beast returned the damage it absorbed, his target's health dropped to under fifty percent, and something unexpected happened.

The mage turned into a bear.

Purple energy rippled along the bear's claws, and the staff itself seemed to have turned into wooden bracers to protect the bear's forepaws. When the giant grizzly roared, Tim saw the purple energy extended to the bear's teeth, and he knew getting bitten would lead to a bad day.

"Hey Boo Boo, I think I saw a pic-a-nic basket," Cassie growled as she slammed her staff into the bear.

Tim gritted his teeth. "Stick with the nose boops."

The bear brought with it a ton of extra damage he hadn't expected. The magical claws ignored Cassie's armor. He switched to Way of the Boulder and cast Who Needs a Shield. The trash fights were supposed to be easy, but the bear lady would've wiped out an unprepared group rather quickly.

They worked together until the woman was lying on her knees before them gasping for air as the last of her hit points bled away.

"It shouldn't be possible." She reached to her neck and ripped the necklace free. "You promised me freedom."

The dragon dropped soundlessly out of the air and bit her in half as it landed. "And so you have it."

Cronos changed from the dragon back to the woman and spat a bit of bloody flesh onto the ground. "I do hate when things get caught in my teeth."

Before Tim could speak, she lifted a single finger to silence him. "If you still wish to face me, meet me in the Garden of Roses, and try not to kill any more of my people along the way."

Cronos turned into a dragon and took flight.

"We killed her? Like we were the ones who bit the lady in half. What is with these bosses and blaming everyone else for their problems?" JaKobi looked at the woman's legs lying on the ground with the guts spilling out and tried not to barf.

Lorelei looked kind of sad. "It's the way of the world. The strong eat the weak."

"Not today." ShadowLily Lifted her fist in the air. "Today, the weak get to take one back."

Tim grinned. "Then let's go win one for the little guy."

As they walked down the path toward the castle, more of the women in white and purple appeared, but none of them tried to bar their way. Instead, they filed in behind the group and followed them toward the castle's Garden of Roses. This was it. They'd almost arrived at the final battle and would be one step closer to getting the Stone of Immoratis for Eternia.

CHAPTER ELEVEN

The Garden of Roses was one of the most beautiful things Tim had ever seen.

Neat beds of purple and white roses formed a football field-sized circle outside the castle. Inside the large outer ring were five smaller circles of roses, each with a massive rosebush at the center. Then three smaller circles without anything at the center, and finally at the precise midpoint of the garden, there was a twenty-foot square of meticulously kept lawn—just the kind of place to set up tables for a party.

Or for a dragon to luxuriate on.

"This puts the botanical gardens to shame. It must've taken generations to cultivate." JaKobi looked at the garden in wonder.

Lorelei huffed. "Or a shit-ton of magic."

"Why would she want to meet us here?" Tim looked around the space. "We're going to mess up her roses."

ShadowLily looked at the plants, then up at the castle. "She doesn't want us to go inside for some reason."

Cassie wiggled her fingers at the castle. "Presto chango."

When nothing happened, the tank shrugged and turned

back to the group. "Seriously, what if it was some little hut magicked up to look like a castle?"

"That would be one hell of a trick." Tim looked over the gardens and up at the castle. "When the fight starts, don't take anything for granted. We already know she's a powerful mage, but Cronos has also proved to be tricky."

JaKobi grunted. "When you can turn into a massive dragon and eat people, I don't think you need to be very tricky. She strikes me as the confrontational type."

"Yet she's part of what happened to the king." Tim let it hang out there.

JaKobi grinned at him. "Touché."

Cassie stepped between them. "Before you guys start to bro down, let's deal with her." She pointed up into the sky.

Cronos spiraled down toward them from above. Each circle she made was wider and slower until she landed on the grass square at the center of the garden. Slowly the dragon blurred, and the evil witch Cronos appeared.

There was no mistaking the change of clothes. Cronos had come ready for battle. Her dark purple robes turned white depending on how she moved, but it wasn't the colors that got Tim's attention. It was the spikes. On her wrist guards, shoulder pads, even the back of her boots. Everything about her outfit spoke of aggression and violence. This wasn't some simple talk to lure them into a trap. This was the final fight.

"Like most adventurers, you weren't smart enough to heed my warnings. Now I must make an example out of you so no one will be so foolish again." Cronos planted her feet and glared at them with hatred.

Tim stepped behind Cassie. "You wrong us with your words, Cronos. You know full well that we wouldn't be here if you hadn't conspired with Isadora against the king. It's time to face the consequences of those actions."

Cronos almost doubled in size as her anger consumed her.

"You lecture me on the consequences of actions. Have you met the nobles? Do they inspire you?"

"About as much as a politician," Cassie whispered.

Tim tried not to laugh or to get distracted. "They might not inspire me, but I also don't go around killing them."

Dark, murderous laughter filled the space. "Is the king not alive? Does he not walk the halls of the castle at this very moment?"

That confirmed Prince Desmond's fears. The king in the castle wasn't the king at all, or at the very least was under Cronos' total control. He doubted they would be able to convince her to part with an antidote or reverse the spell so they were down to their last option, kill the evil bitch and hope for the best.

"We both know he doesn't." Tim let the words hang between them for a moment so she could feel the weight of them. "If it's not us, it will be another group of adventurers. Now that Desmond knows the truth of it, you'll never see peace."

Cronos screamed, "Peace is a lie." She turned away from them and walked to create some distance. "If you insist on a fight, I am feeling rather peckish."

With a roar, she changed from a woman back into a dragon.

"Oh shit." Tim looked into the monster's eyes and wondered if this was how a seal felt when the water shifted beneath them as a great white went in for the kill from below.

Cronos rose into the sky, and Tim called, "Get ready for it."

The dragon turned and banked in a lazy circle, belching out fire. The only areas untouched were the grass at the center of the garden and the center of each smaller circle. Flames consumed everything else as Cronos continued to fly in lazy arcs across the entire space.

"Into the grass." It might not be the best place for them to go, but it was the closest, and it was a safe zone so Tim made the call.

The group piled into the grass square as Cronos finished her circle of flames. Tim looked around the battlefield, trying to figure out what he missed. Would it be better for them to try and pile inside the smallest circles or maybe the larger circles with single plants at the center? He didn't know yet, the fight was too new, but he knew those areas would come into play eventually.

The dragon quickly spiraled higher into the air and descended at the grass square like a falling rock. The only choice they had to make now was to jump into the flames or try and absorb the damage from the boss's attack.

"Everyone stack on Cassie!" Tim squawked as he ran toward the tank.

They dove into a pile under Cassie's protective shielding as Cronos slammed into the grass. The shockwave was enough to leave Tim feeling woozy, but he was on his feet in an instant. There wasn't time to check if they had negative status effects so Tim cast a mass Cleanse and followed it up with a trio of Healing Orb. With everyone's health moving in the right direction, he felt better about the situation.

They couldn't afford to make that mistake a second time.

"My vote is next time we stay out of the grass. Find a way to make that happen," Cassie snapped as she moved to engage the boss.

She was right. He was the mechanics guy. At least they weren't facing a full-on dragon anymore. As soon as Cronos hit the ground, she turned back into a woman. Being in human form didn't seem to make the witch any less formidable as her magical claws made her as deadly as Freddy Krueger rocking two gloves.

Cassie and Cronos tangled, staff against magical claws. The fire trapping them in the rectangle of grass slowly extinguished, and Tim knew it was time for the group to get moving.

"Get us close to one of those big circles." Tim cast Hex of the Shattered Beast and followed it with Curse of Sacrifice.

Cassie didn't waste any time as she used her attacks to position the boss. A good tank was worth its weight in gold, and watching Cassie work now was like watching Michelangelo paint the Sistine Chapel. Trailing behind the pair like an artist of death, ShadowLily wove a deadly tapestry of destruction with her daggers. The assassin was pushing herself this fight, and the numbers spoke for themselves.

Traditionally it was easier for ranged DPS to top the charts. A ranged player could get into optimal position faster, and they normally didn't have to move as much to dodge attacks. One of the biggest luxuries of playing from range was the ability to see the entire battlefield and cut loose until they had to move. When the DPS played up close, they moved as much as the tank while doing the same DPS as the players standing still.

The mist slayer handled the challenge like a pro. No one was going to tell her she couldn't top the charts on every fight. It meant pushing herself to the limit. As Tim watched her work, he felt inspired. She was a fantastic player, and they were lucky to have her in their group. Not to mention it kind of made him hot seeing her dart around wreaking havoc in those tight leather pants.

Like having his very own half-elf Mila Jovovich.

As the group moved closer to the circle with the rose bush in the center, the top of the bush started to wiggle. Tim didn't have to be a deep thinker to know movement normally meant nasty things were about to happen. So far, his ideas for this fight led them from one spot of trouble right into another. They wouldn't be able to win this fight eating the damage from Cronos' slam, the fire, and whatever the rose bush was about to do to them.

The rose bush burst from the ground. It was some kind of plant monster wearing the bush as a hat. Loose roots dangled around the face of the mandrake-like creature as it opened its mouth. Instead of a scream that could've stunned them, a stream of thorns sprayed from the creature's open mouth dealing damage to the entire party. The thorns also applied a DOT to the group.

Tim was about to tell Cassie to back up when the rose bush creature slipped back into the ground. Cassie barely noticed the increase so she didn't start moving the boss away from the circle on her own. The damage they were taking right now, even with the DOT, was easily handled by Hydrate, but if the DOT stacked and they stayed put it would become a problem.

What were they going to do?

They needed to find a way to stay close enough to the circle to run in when Cronos turned back into a dragon but far enough away not to trigger the AOE attack. It was a tricky tightrope to walk, but they could do it if they tightened things up. This was the final fight. Of course, it was going to be hard.

Tim's Hex Beast slammed into the boss, but she hardly even flinched. He wanted to cast Behold My Power but couldn't risk wasting it if Cronos would change back to her dragon form soon. Instead, he settled for casting another round of Healing Orb as he prepared to tell Cassie what he wanted her to do next.

She was going to be so pissed.

The bush started shaking again, and there wasn't going to be time to get out of the way. His mana was dipping with the early damage they took from Cronos' opening salvo and again when he made the mistake of asking Cassie to get close to the rose bush. Not knowing if there was another way out or if it would even work at all, Tim cast Disturbance and hoped for the best. When the spell hit the bush, it stopped moving.

The real question was for how long?

Never one to let an opportunity go to waste, Tim called, "Cassie, let's move closer to the center again."

Until they had an active bush to test the range of the attack, there was no reason to get her riled up with useless commands. For now, he'd settle for not getting hit with the DOT again, and then he could explain to her what happened when Cronos did her dragon thing. At some point, they'd have to make a run for the rose bush and the protection of the circle, but until then it was easier to stay away.

"We just got out of the damn center," the shadow dancer grumbled as she started to move.

Tim laughed as he reapplied Curse of Giving. "Tell me about it."

Cronos roared as she hit seventy-five percent and her body shifted back into dragon form.

"Everyone in the circle," Tim called as he ran.

Cassie grunted. "Into the circle, out of the circle, make up your damn mind already."

Cronos took flight as they entered the ring, lighting the garden on fire again as she flew in a slow circle. While the fire raged outside, the rose bush creature seemed content to stay below the surface.

"At least we got to rest for a minute." Tim watched his mana bar replenish as he filled Cassie in on what they needed to try during the next phase.

Cronos decided they'd had too much time to rest. As she reached the pinnacle of her flight, she again descended with all the deadly power of a meteorite. When she hit the grass, the ground quaked, and Tim was grateful they skipped out on a big chunk of damage.

When the fire in the center of the area died out, the ground beneath his feet pulsed red.

Red means dead.

"Everyone out." Tim made the call as he started running.

When JaKobi didn't move, Tim tapped Cassie on the shoulder. "Get him for me."

Her chain came out, and she yanked the ember wizard forward as the circle burst into flames.

Tim looked at the circle for a moment, trying to decide what they should do next. "That's our enrage timer. As long as we don't burn two of the circles at the same time, we have four more chances to knock out the last seventy-five percent."

"Just tell me where to stand." Cassie ran toward Cronos and made sure she had the witch's full attention before she started moving her toward the circle Tim pointed out.

"When you see that bush start to shake, back it up a few feet." Not eating an attack was important this time, but not as important as making sure they had the right distance down for the rest of the fight.

Lorelei broke out in peals of laughter. "I kinda like it when a girl's bush has a little shake. That's my call to move in, not to back it up."

JaKobi shot a beam of sunlight at the boss. "Preach it, sister."

Tim tried not to think about what these two got up to before he knew them and tried to focus on the fight. He quickly reapplied Curse of Giving and cast Behold My Power. From there, he dropped into a holding pattern. He didn't know when it would happen, but the second phase normally added a little something extra to the fight. While the wrinkle hadn't shown up yet, he was determined to be ready for it when it did.

Cassie moved the boss toward the next circle, and when the bush started to shake, she moved slightly farther away. The rose bush stopped shaking, and just like that, they found the perfect distance. The group quickly fell into the guileless rhythm of battle. Each of them worked as hard as they could to push Cronos to the next phase as quickly as possible.

Tim watched as the boss' health dipped to sixty-five percent, then sixty. They still hadn't been blasted by an extra attack, and he was getting worried. Not having an extra mechanic pop up didn't feel right. Something big was coming, and it would be coming soon.

Cronos hit fifty-five percent, and now his nerves were simply dancing.

The boss' magical claws started to turn into real ones, and Tim knew they were about to get scorched again. This time they were in the perfect position to move into the circle when the fire started. So far they'd done everything right, and when the dragon took off, they would step out of the circle into phase three of the fight.

This time they would come out with full health and mana and higher spirits. Maybe he'd been wrong, and they had this fight under control all along.

Then disaster struck.

Cronos broke free from Cassie, stormed into the middle of their party, and spun in a circle using her massive tail to send all of them flying in different directions. The lucky ones got knocked closer to the safe zone, but the unlucky were scattered further away from a haven. Tim made a mental note that if they survived this, to change their positioning so JaKobi would get knocked closer to safety instead of farther away.

The ember wizard was the slowest member of their group, which of course meant the mechanic's first use knocked him the farthest away. That didn't stop JaKobi from leaping to his feet and putting every inch of his strength and dexterity to use as he rushed toward safety. Tim watched him for a moment and began his mad dash toward safety, hoping his friend would be fast enough to make it.

"Lorelei, use an interrupt." Tim almost just shouted interrupt, but at the last second, he remembered everyone might cast simultaneously and settled on the closest player with the longest range.

The spirit archer executed the interrupt as Cassie stepped

into safety. The rose bush monster stayed hidden as Shadow-Lily and Lorelei entered the circle of roses.

Hearing the fire roaring behind him as it drew closer was the most horrible sound Tim ever heard. It was like death was screaming at him, and no matter how fast he ran away it was always getting closer. At least he wasn't trapped in a burning building. All he had to do was make it to the circle instead of deciding whether to jump.

Tim activated Quick Feet, putting on a burst of speed that left the ember wizard trailing in his dust.

Entering the protective circle of roses, Tim turned back to watch JaKobi. "Run, Forressst!"

"Damn, that's cold." Lorelei snickered.

JaKobi tried not to smile as he put everything he had into running. "I'd totally trade a box of chocolates for a movement spell."

"You don't need one." Cassie threw her chain, and it wrapped around JaKobi's waist as the flames hit his heels.

With a solid yank, she pulled the ember wizard out of the fire and into safety. Tim got to work healing. As soon as JaKobi was at full health, Tim pulled up his user interface to look over the entire group's status. Everyone was at full health, and the boss was sitting under fifty percent. The new wrinkle seemed to be a knockback before the flames. That particular skill was easy enough to manage, but there would be a new wrinkle coming out of this phase. There always was.

Probably something that's going to make me run. I hate that shit.

"JaKobi, switch places with Lorelei during the next phase. We need you getting knocked closer even if it means you stop DPS early to get in position." Tim looked at the group and shrugged. "That's all I've got until we see what the boss has in store for us."

Cassie pointed as Cronos started rising higher in the sky, preparing for her slam. "Get ready for it because she's coming."

When Cronos hit the grass, the ground shook, their protective circle burned away, and it turned into an attack as they fled. The new twist didn't present itself right away, and Cassie stood in front of the group ready to intercept the boss.

Tim felt super tense, but maybe that was his default reaction to doing well. It was like he was always waiting for the other shoe to drop.

Sometimes it never did.

Cronos charged toward their group with her magical claws extended, ready to rip them to pieces. Cassie rushed in from the side, cut off the boss's charge, and started moving her into position. Tim cast Curse of Giving and Curse of Sacrifice as Cassie led the boss toward the next circle.

A glance to Tim's left confirmed JaKobi was in the right place. Things were going smoothly, and with their adjusted formation, they should be able to make it into the circle during the phase change without any last-second heroics. The way things were going, they might even make it out of this fight with a circle to spare. After losing their first battle with Isadora, they were playing at the top of their game.

Tim cast three Healing Orb to spread Hydrate, and started interchanging Curse of Sacrifice and Divine Light. Cronos hit forty-five percent, then forty. At thirty-nine percent, she started to glow. At thirty-five, a circle formed under the boss' feet and let out intermittent bolts of energy they had to dodge. So now they had their first real big movement problem to deal with.

"Oh fuck," ShadowLily swore as she rolled forward at the wrong time and right into one of Cronos' energy attacks.

Who Needs a Shield was the first thing Tim cast. As soon as he saw the spell take hold, he flipped the target of his Way of the Boulder stance from Cassie to ShadowLily. The next five seconds disappeared in a flash as he did damage to the boss.

When the mist slayer had her full health, it was easy enough to flip his stance back to Cassie.

A round of Healing Orb topped off the group, and it was like the mistake never happened.

Letting out a deep breath, Tim looked at Cronos' health and realized she was at twenty-eight percent. While he'd been stressing out, the rest of his group had kept working. The trust they had in his ability to pull them out of the fire was humbling.

I won't ever tell them how close they came to death.

At twenty-five percent, something new happened.

Cronos ran to the grassy area and started to cast a spell.

"I have a bad feeling about this," Tim shouted as they started moving toward the circle of protection.

Cassie grunted. "You always have a bad feeling. Try lightening up a little, dude."

"Don't worry, be happy," JaKobi sang.

ShadowLily slapped him on the back of the head. "Not the right time."

"Winds of the East, I call upon you!" Cronos shouted as she pointed her hands up to the heavens.

A tornado formed from the tip of her finger and grew before doubling almost instantly and again equally quickly. Tim didn't think the rose bush trick would protect them from this so they had to wait for the spell to take effect and find some way to use the aftermath to their advantage.

One by one, the tornado sucked them off their feet and pulled them into the grassy area. Cronos continued her shift into a dragon as the tornado spat them out at the corner farthest away from the three remaining circles. As they landed on the ground, the dragon took flight.

"Run!" Tim cried.

Cassie didn't hesitate. She picked up JaKobi and slung him over one shoulder before taking off. "I might have to talk with

Roberto about how many burritos you've been eating." She slapped his ass and kept moving.

"Hey, you can't gain weight in this game." The ember wizard bounced along on Cassie's shoulder.

They were going to make it. Everything was going to be just fine.

The tornado pulled JaKobi and Cassie back toward the grass area while the rest of them kept running free. Tim watched them land before turning in time to see ShadowLily stun the rose bush creature in the circle they'd been heading for. Lorelei made it into the circle next, and he stumbled inside a moment later.

Cassie and JaKobi were separated, and there was no way the tank could reach him and run to safety. She sprinted toward the next big circle hoping she'd be fast enough not to be deep-fried.

"JaKobi, get in the nearest big circle, don't forget to interrupt." Tim turned toward Cassie. "You gotta get in one of the small ones."

Cassie slid to a stop outside the closest big circle, her toes inches away. "A little heads-up would've been nice."

"Just trying to make sure your boyfriend is safe," Tim quipped.

"Why do I have to run way over there when this one is right here?" Cassie scuffed her toes on the edge.

"That circle is the only thing stopping us from having to get back in the grass with Cronos," Tim shouted back.

The choice was up to Cassie, but they would all know if she made the wrong one and they had to start the fight over. If she got in the small circle and it didn't save her, all the blame was on him. She got in the circle.

It was the safest bet.

"I better not die a fiery death," Cassie grumbled as she glared at Tim.

The flames washed over Cassie's area and didn't touch her. Then they moved past their group and JaKobi. Thankfully Cassie didn't make the selfish play, and they had their safety net in place if they failed to kill Cronos during this phase. If they somehow managed to squeak their way into a fifth phase, the boss would probably be enraged. The last thing he wanted to deal with was an enraged dragon, so they had to kill her now.

Stomp, dead. Fire breath, dead. Tail whip, dead. Razor teeth, dead. That was a whole lotta death and not a lot of winning.

This wasn't the time to start worrying about what would happen if they fucked up. It was time to focus up and see this fight through to the rightful conclusion. A Blue Dagger Society win. Cronos was sitting at twenty-four percent health, and all they needed to do was find a way to maintain their DPS.

They didn't have to improve, only hold the status quo.

The flames disappeared, and so did their protection. Cronos did what any cornered animal would do and found the weakest target and tried to take them out first. JaKobi tried to put up a wall of flames, but the boss ran through it.

At the last instant, Cassie managed to get her chain around Cronos' leg, and that one simple action might've saved their asses. JaKobi only took half of the swipe intended to end his life, which meant he was down but not out.

As long as Tim could reach him in time.

Heals poured out of Tim as if he existed only for this moment. Seeing his best friend lying on the ground in a pool of his blood tended to have that kind of effect on him. This was one of those never leave a man behind moments. He was willing to risk it all to save his friend. They were going to win this fight together.

How very poetic.

At least he didn't only have to heal his buddy back to full health. Tim got to deal out a little retribution while he was doing it. Most healers would have to wait for their friends to do the damage, but he didn't have that problem.

He switched his stance from Cassie to JaKobi and repeatedly blasted Cronos with Curse of Sacrifice, only stopping when the ember wizard was at one hundred percent. Then he switched his stance back to Cassie and duplicated the process.

Switching the target of his stances was a nice feature, and his DPS while JaKobi was out of the fight might be enough to keep them on track. The light under Cronos' feet was flashing again, and now she sent out multiple bursts of energy every time she moved. With a wave of one hand, the witch called forth swarms of bees. They flew through the garden in solid swarms that the group had to dodge or be overwhelmed. Now they not only had to dodge the bursts of electrical energy but roving clouds of stinging death.

"I fucking hate bees." Lorelei fired a flaming arrow into one of the swarms with no effect.

Tim pointed at Cronos. "Kill her, and they all go away."

"Now you're speaking my language." The spirit archer ran forward, dove into a roll, and came up firing as if her very life depended on it.

Maybe it did.

Cassie had the boss now and was dragging her into position as the rest of them put everything they had into destroying the rest of her health. The bees swarming around were slowing them down, but there was nothing they could do about it. Life turned into a deadly game of dodge bee, which wasn't nearly as fun as dodgeball.

If you can dodge a bee, you can dodge a dragon.

Cronos's health dropped to fifteen percent, and she thrashed around. The change back into her dragon form was happening whether she wanted it to or not. They hit ten percent, then nine. This time the dragon didn't fly into the air but attacked them much more physically.

What big teeth you have.

Watching their tank's health fall like a rock gave him palpitations, but Tim kept on casting. He blew all his defensive cooldowns and let life devolve into a world that involved only two things, Healing Orb and Curse of Sacrifice.

At one percent, Cronos stopped taking damage.

Her dragon form fell away, and in its place was a beaten and broken woman. She looked up at Tim with a sad smile. "It seems even I can learn new lessons. It's too bad learning humility is such a kick in the teeth."

The last of her health started slowly ticking away. Then something amazing happened.

Eternia appeared floating down from the heavens. Cronos' health stopped dropping as the goddess extended her hand to help her to her feet. "Your time in this realm is at an end. Let me help you find peace in the next."

"You do me a great honor, Goddess, and it's not one I truly deserve." Cronos turned her eyes toward the adventurers. "Maybe there is one thing I can do for you before I go that will tip the scales of fate in my favor."

The goddess nodded in acceptance, and Cronos snapped her fingers. With that simple gesture complete, Eternia reached out, taking a firm grip of Cronos's arm, and they rose into the heavens together. When Tim turned his eyes back to the spot they'd been standing in, there was a beautiful golden chest.

It was loot time.

CHAPTER TWELVE

"So what was all that about?" Cassie waved toward where Eternia and Cronos disappeared together. "It's not a lot of help to wave and fly off."

Tim looked up into the heavens. "Goddess things, and as to your second question, I guess we'll find out."

ShadowLily put an arm around his waist. "That's about as helpful as Cronos' last words."

It was true. His words were worth as much as dust in the wind. He didn't know what Eternia was up to and had even less idea what Cronos tried to reveal. The answer they were seeking could always be in the loot chest. It had been a while since they found items inside a chest, but it had happened. This situation might not be any different.

"Maybe it's in the loot," Tim ventured.

"In the loot, you say?" JaKobi ran forward.

The ember wizard made it about ten steps before Cassie's chain wrapped around his waist and yanked him back. "Not a chance, mister."

JaKobi bowed and moved out of the way. "It's only fair with you saving my ass all the time."

"Don't you forget it." Cassie moved forward and laid her hand on the chest.

The tank pulled her hand back, leapt on top of the chest, and triumphantly hefted her bō staff in the air. "Necklace of the Dragon, it has magical resistances up the ass."

"Keeping it classy, as usual." Lorelei snickered as she moved to the chest.

The spirit archer turned toward them, taking a moment to process the piece of gear she received. "Mythical Wrist Guard of Tempted Fate. The item stores charges for every critical attack. When it reaches five charges, it's full, and the special effect activates. One of three things can happen when it does. Nothing, doubles my next attack's damage, or triples my next attack's damage but also takes fifteen percent of my health."

It was an amazing item but a risky one to use in key fights. The last thing they needed was for her special ability to trigger and kill her before he could get a heal off. On the other hand, he loved the idea of getting a supercharged attack, and there was a two out of three chance that nothing bad happened. Sure, it was risky, but it was the kind of risk that would pay off as long as he could keep up with the additional healing.

Hope my loot is as cool as hers.

"I think it's awesome," Tim blurted as everyone was thinking about the ramifications and the bonuses.

Lorelei grinned. "Damn straight it's awesome. The real question is how many times will it activate in a fight."

"Hope you brought your A-game because you're going to need it." ShadowLily nudged Tim as she moved toward the chest.

The mist slayer looked up a few moments later. "Not nearly as cool as Lorelei's, but I got a new pair of boots, and they boost all the right things in all the right places."

JaKobi glanced over his shoulder to make sure Tim wasn't in a big hurry and placed his hand on the chest. "Gloves of the

Blazing Sun. Boosts my newest spell and increases my stats. Nothing to complain about."

Tim knew the feeling well. It was nice to get an upgrade, but after seeing someone score a piece of epic loot, it was hard to get excited about a simple upgrade. Not that they didn't appreciate any upgrade, it was just some drops were more memorable than others. After his pants, he was due for a good roll.

Moving toward the chest, Tim tried to keep his hopes in check. "Hey, did anyone get anything besides loot?"

When four "no's" came back, Tim put his hand on the chest, thinking about when they'd find out what last surprise Cronos left for them.

Item Received: Dragon Hyde Jerkin

Dragons aren't easily killed in battle, and items made from their remains are even rarer. It might seem like a waste to use some of the most valuable material in the world to make a simple jerkin, but for Jalen the Clumsy, it was a simple matter of survival. He needed the extra protection and had the money to pay for the best. His legacy now lives on with you.

Hopefully, with a little less falling.

Increases all base stats by two and all secondary stats by one.

Tim held his breath as he looked over the description again. Sure, an additional plus one to his base stats wasn't all that big of a deal, but the increase to his secondary stats was amazing. This was the first time he'd ever received an item that increased those stats. It had been a while since he'd even thought of them at all. There were so many skills he had to increase that finding ways to up his secondary stats had fallen to the wayside.

With the update, Tim's Endurance hit thirty, and he received a small boost to damage reduction and a slight bump to his overall health. He wasn't as squishy as he used to be with the new armor pieces and increased endurance. Now he was turning into a healer who could stand in the thick of things without fear of dying to a single wayward hit.

"I got a new jerkin, with an increase to my secondary stats." Tim looked in the rest of his inventory to see if he received anything else and came up with bupkiss.

JaKobi looked incredulous. "Bro, nothing increases those stats. What an awesome drop."

Tim gave him a high five. "Thanks, man!"

"No information on the king?" Lorelei brought them all back to reality.

Tim shook his head. "Nope. Looks like we'll have to see if anything is waiting for us inside the castle."

"They better not force some random fight on us, like Cronos wasn't the real boss," Cassie grumbled as she led the way to the castle.

Smiling as he thought about what the fiery little tank said, Tim wouldn't have put a trick like that past the cruel developers that loved to taunt them with twists and turns in the story. This time the twist of another boss appearing didn't feel quite right. They defeated Cronos, and she'd promised them answers with the last words she spoke on this plane of existence. There had to be something they were missing.

"Let's get to the castle and find out." Tim reached out and stopped Cassie from taking off at a jog. "No running."

The rose garden faded away behind them as they worked their way back to the front of the castle. As they returned to the main path, the castle doors opened, and a woman walked out carrying a man in her arms like an infant.

Tim looked at ShadowLily, and she shrugged. His heart was racing. There was no way it could be who he thought it was, yet it wouldn't make any sense for it to be anyone but the king.

If this was King Rasmus, who was with Prince Desmond at the castle?

"The Lady Cronos bid me return King Rasmus to you before sealing the castle grounds." The woman who must have magically enhanced strength walked forward and placed the king in Cassie's outstretched arms.

"With my duty done, let me show you to the borders of our land." Clapping her hands together, the woman created a portal and motioned for them to step inside.

Tim looked at Cassie carrying the vulnerable king in her arms. "I'll go first."

"Better let me." ShadowLily didn't have to say that she could survive a solo fight a lot longer than he could.

"I'm right behind you." Every fighter needed a good healer.

Tim followed her through the portal with Lorelei and JaKobi right behind him. Cassie brought up the rear with the king in her arms.

As he stepped out of the portal, Tim realized all his fears had been for nothing. The clearing they stood in was free of enemies and traps. The carriage was waiting for them, and Grant was already holding the door open. Cassie moved past the others with the sleeping King Rasmus held easily in her arms.

Tim cast Cleanse, but it didn't seem to have any effect on the king. If they wanted any real answers, they had to get the man back to Eternia and see if she could do more to heal him than he could. Once they revived the king, they could start planning the best way to help Prince Desmond get rid of the imposter.

Grant's eyes widened as the tank approached. "Is that who I think it is?"

Cassie grunted with effort as she lifted the king into the carriage. "Get us back to the inn as quickly as you can."

Tim turned to see the woman from the castle had followed them to the entrance. "Thank you for returning the king to us."

"Thank you for setting us free." The woman stepped back into the portal.

The shimmering border that marked the entrance to Cronos' land faded and left them looking at an empty forest as if the place had never existed. *Magic was so fucking cool.* Tim joined the others in the carriage.

"Let's get out of here." He tapped the top of the carriage, and it started to move.

"You weren't lying when you said this was the best food in the kingdom." Rasmus dipped his fork into some corned beef hash and ran it through some egg yolk before lifting it to his mouth.

Tim nodded at the comment as Joe and Roberto beamed with pride. "I'm telling you if my job were just to eat here twice a day, I'd be the happiest man in the world."

Eternia watched them all from her place by the fire. "It won't be long now before Desmond reaches out to us. You have to be ready."

ShadowLily lifted a glass of rumpleberry juice. "We're ready."

"The fight against the shapeshifter will be unlike anything you've ever faced. To come out victorious, you must be able to face your fears." Eternia smiled. "If you win, it will be a victory for the ages."

King Rasmus sipped his juice. "While you fight, I'll secure the stone for the goddess. So regardless of the outcome, before the fight is over, I'll have the stone safely into Eternia's hands."

Cassie ripped pieces off a giant cinnamon roll. "Just one more fight, and we finally get to take the battle back to Vitaria."

"This time, we'll be ready." Eternia stood. "Thank you, brave adventurers, for all that you've done. Let me bless you before you leave."

A wave of energy washed over the entire inn, and Tim felt refreshed as if he'd woken up from the best night's sleep he ever had. "Blue Dagger for life."

The cheer echoed across the room.

"Father, I have great news." Prince Desmond ran into the throne room. "The vile witch Cronos has been defeated."

The king stood and scowled with what Desmond could only describe as pure loathing. "Then we should honor the brave adventurers with medals and maybe something from the family vault."

He knew what the king was doing. Ever since the pretender had murdered his mother, he'd been searching for excuses to force Desmond into opening the vault. That was why he'd released Desmond from prison. So far, the prince had been able to politely refuse, knowing the imposter would never admit he couldn't open the vault himself.

The time for pretending was over.

"I think that would be a great idea," Prince Desmond replied smoothly. "Previously, I promised them the Stone of Immoratis. It seems like just the reward to honor their great victory."

The creature pretending to be Rasmus let out a low growl, and a bit of drool slipped down his chin before he was able to compose himself. "They deserve no less. Bring these adventurers before me and let us honor them as the heroes they are."

"It will be as you command, Father." Desmond swept from the room as if carrying out the creature's wish was his greatest desire.

Soon he would have his revenge for his mother's death.

Desmond wouldn't rest until the thing that killed her was dead and burned to ash. As he walked from the castle back to the temple, and the only place he felt truly safe, the prince let out the first smile he'd had in days. The crisis was almost over, and they would soon be able to find their way back to a new version of normal.

"I'm going to miss you, Mom." Desmond whispered a prayer to the goddess, asking her to guide his mother's spirit toward the light and make sure she was as happy in the afterlife as she was with them.

CHAPTER THIRTEEN

Prince Desmond met them outside the earl's gate. "Cherished adventurers, please allow me to join you as the captain of your honor guard and escort you safely to the castle."

Tim heard the words honor guard and thought prisoners was a better description for their trip than guests. "Thank you, Prince Desmond. We would be thrilled to have you join us." He held out his hand, giving the prince permission to enter their carriage.

When he sees who's inside, it's going to blow his mind.

"Grant, follow the king's men, no detours." He hoped the way he phrased it let the driver know the seriousness of their situation.

"Wouldn't dream of doing anything else." The carriage driver tipped his cap and closed the door.

Once the carriage was moving again, Tim turned his attention back to the prince. "You know all of us, but you haven't met our newest assistant."

"Assistant my ass." King Rasmus removed his hood. "I might owe you my life, but I'm still the fucking king."

Tim bowed his head in subservience. "Your Majesty."

"Dad." Prince Desmond reached out, unable to believe it. When his hand touched the king, he broke down in tears. "I have terrible news."

Rasmus moved swiftly, pulling his son into a fierce hug. "The Goddess Eternia told me everything. We will deal with the thing that killed your mother, and then we'll lay your mother to rest properly."

There was quiet determination in Rasmus' voice, but it was easy enough for all of them to see he was heartbroken. The burden of leadership didn't give the king the option of indulging in his grief until the kingdom was secure. Being sad didn't keep people fed or the forces of evil at bay.

It was heartbreaking to watch, yet the king earned Tim's deepest respect at that moment. A true leader would always put the needs of his subjects in front of their own. Tim was excited to see what the king would be like once he returned to his throne.

"I look forward to seeing her off properly." Prince Desmond's back straightened. "Now, tell me what the six of you have planned and how I can help."

Cassie slapped Prince Desmond on the shoulder. "You know, I was on the fence about you, but you're a pretty good guy."

Lorelei rolled her eyes. "What she meant to say is we're sorry for your loss."

"And happy to reunite the two of you," ShadowLily added smoothly.

The king chuckled as he watched his son's head move from person to person, trying to keep up. "I can see you've had your hands full dealing with these adventurers."

"I've been willing to indulge them because they don't only solve problems but generate sensational taxes for the kingdom." Desmond looked pointedly at Tim. "Yes, I know who Mr. Applebottom works for."

"Ah, I thought that inn looked familiar." The king slammed his fist into his leg. "The Blue Dagger. It sure looks different, and the food is so much better than anything else in the kingdom."

Turning back to the prince the king smiled widely. "I can't even explain to you the delights. We'll have to go together."

"Eat in the city? You're not going to have the chef come to the castle?" Desmond looked flabbergasted.

The king nodded. "I've been away from my people for too long. How can I ever hope to rule them if I can't understand them?"

"That carrot cake didn't hurt, right?" Cassie nudged Rasmus in the ribs, realized what she'd done, and scooted away. "Ah, sorry, Your Majesty."

The king waved dismissively. "Think nothing of it. It's been a long time since I've spoken with anyone who didn't constantly kiss my ass. It's quite refreshing in small doses." He raised an eyebrow as he waited to see if she got the point.

Cassie relaxed. "So what do you say we fill the prince in on the plan and get ready to rock and roll."

"Rock and roll?" Rasmus looked at them quizzically.

Tim grinned. "It's something we say where we're from when we're ready to kick some ass."

"That's something I can understand." The king leaned back in his seat and looked at his son. "Get ready. You're going to enjoy this."

Desmond looked at the assembled adventurers with excitement. "Of that, I have no doubt."

The shapeshifter looked down on the assembled group of adventurers with a loathing smile.

Prince Desmond stood boldly before the throne. "Father, may I present to you the Blue Dagger Society. Slayers of Isadora and Cronos, saviors of our kingdom."

If the thing pretending to be the king was impressed, he gave no indication. "These are the ones that slew Cronos? I almost find it unbelievable."

The court gasped at his words. They thought they were coming to see a reward ceremony, and that clearly wasn't going to happen.

"Leave us!" The king roared from the throne. "I wish to attend to these slayers of witches myself."

As the courtesans and their guards filed out, the king looked at Desmond. "Shouldn't you be fetching their reward?"

"Originally, I hoped to see them honored, but you are right, Father. I will go and get the stone for them immediately." Desmond looked toward the doors of the throne room as they were sealed shut.

There's no getting out of this now.

Tim wasn't one to miss too many tricks. The pretender had locked them all inside the throne room together. If they'd ever questioned whether a fight was coming their way, they had their answer. How smart the both of them thought they were, each setting traps for the other when it had always been inevitable they would end up right here.

He bowed low and addressed the throne. "Your Majesty, before you see to our promised restitution, I wondered if I could beg one last boon from you."

"I grow tired of these endless demands upon my time." The imposter smiled, and his lips pulled wider, showing an extra row of teeth. "But speak your request, lest my son thinks me uncouth."

Tim bowed low again. "Thank you for your kindness. I

have but a single request, and I hope you will honor it. If you could spare the good Prince Desmond for a few moments, I'd appreciate it if he could escort our servant to the temple? He's a huge fan of the architecture, and if I have to listen to him gripe about not seeing it the entire ride home, I'll lose my mind."

"Go." The king smiled. "I do enjoy a request that requires zero effort on my behalf. Open the doors," he roared. "But only Desmond and the servant leave."

Prince Desmond stopped in front of Tim and shook his hand. "Thank you for your service to the crown."

"I expect your father will fully compensate me for the risk." Tim smiled back, hoping he could wrangle a few more properties from the crown. "Please see that our servant is well-treated until we return."

"You have my word." The prince took the real king's arm and led him from the room.

They have work to do, but so do we.

The shapeshifter rose from the throne, shed his Rasmus-like skin, and stood to its full height. He was ten feet tall now, with hands and feet that looked more like claws for tearing into meat versus something to walk on. His mouth was wider than it should have been and lined with teeth so sharp it would've made Jaws jealous.

Now that his façade had lifted, the shapeshifter sighed. "I hate wearing that thing. It's so restricting."

Tim felt laughter roll up from his belly before he could stop it. The comment seemed so wrong for the moment, yet he loved it. It was like something from one of his favorite movies.

He grinned up into the devilish face of the shapeshifter and gave a little bow. "I'm happy to see your true face finally. I was getting tired of the Edgar suit."

"Mock me if you must, little human, but tonight I feast on the bones of adventurers, and tomorrow I take the stone to resurrect my mistress." The shifter smiled, knowing they had no way out of the throne room.

Cassie snorted. "You think we're scared to be in here with you? You should be scared to be in here with us."

Without another word, she charged into the battle.

"Oh shit, there goes the neighborhood." JaKobi fired his sunbeam with a grin.

Cassie and the shapeshifter clashed together. The creature used its claws and extra-long arms like spears as it tried to murder the tank. She took a few hits, and her health started to plummet. It didn't take long for Tim to figure out the boss had a stackable DOT titled Drain that was applied every time he hit the tank.

Cleanse worked to remove the stacks, but by the time he cast Curse of Giving, Curse of Sacrifice, and Hex of the Shattered Beast on the boss, the stacks were right back to where he had to be concerned. If they wanted to win this fight, the theme of the night would be casting Cleanse almost as often as his heals.

"Anyone not named Cassie who gets the DOT on them, call it out." Tim watched his Golden Retriever charge at the shapeshifter and burst from his back covered in red mist before disappearing.

The game was right, it was a little crazy for him to have the world's friendliest animal as his Hex Beast, but he couldn't help himself. Every time he used the spell, he loved watching the dog appear and return some of the damage done to Cassie back to the boss. There was something rewarding in working together with an animal, even if his pet was a spirit manifestation.

When ShadowLily entered the fray, Tim's need to cast Cleanse increased dramatically. The mist slayer wasn't taking as many hits as Cassie, but her damage reduction and health pool weren't nearly as big as the tank's. He kept his eyes flickering to her because there was no way she could call out every single hit. At least for the time being, Lorelei and JaKobi weren't taking any damage so things were going relatively well in the mana department.

At ninety percent, there was a random twitch of the boss's shoulder, and Tim cast his interrupt. It might have been a mistake to use it this early, but he didn't want to see what the boss' special attack was unless they had to. With the attack stopped, the boss was stunned for a second. Then he cast a buff on himself.

Incinerator: One hundred percent increase to fire damage.

Fire damage? He hasn't cast a spell yet.

As if on cue, the shapeshifter reached into the pouch at his waist and threw five golden coins into the room. As they flew from the creature's hand, they grew in size and landed on the floor. A pulsing red circle appeared around them.

The only thing Tim could think of as an explanation was the coins were landmines, but instead of popping in the air and releasing the ultimate destruction, these would release their inferno in a column of energy.

With the boss' fire attacks buffed, hitting one of those traps might as well have been a death sentence.

"Landmines!" he cried, hoping everyone had the good sense to stay away from the pulsing red circles on the ground.

Ten seconds later the mines went off, and gouts of blue flame launched into the air like erupting volcanoes. The flames faded away, but the scorch marks on the floor were still pulsing red, letting him know they would do damage if they stepped on those spots. Scorch marks weren't only for esthetics.

"Watch your feet," Tim called as he saw JaKobi's health plummet.

The ember wizard was busy putting out a fire on his robes.

"You know, it feels a lot better when I'm the one doing the burning."

"I bet it does." Tim splashed him with a Healing Orb and cast a group Cleanse.

The group Cleanse was the right spell to use if something affected three or more of them. Otherwise, it was cheaper to cast the single-target version. In this instance, it saved him time from having to check the two women's stats as he turned his attention back to bolster their health.

Sometimes healing felt like running a cost-benefit analysis.

They cruised past eighty-five percent health, and Tim cast Behold My Power. It felt like the right time to drop his hardest-hitting spell. The shapeshifter already tried to initiate a special attack and buffed himself so it felt too early for a phase change. Stranger things had happened to Tim in fights, but that much coming at them all at once felt like overkill. The fights should get harder as they went on, not blast you out of the water before you had a chance to swim.

When the boss hit eighty percent, Tim watched intently to see if he saw the same twitch as before. "ShadowLily, interrupt!"

The mist slayer broke off her attack instantly and cast her interrupt. God, he loved playing with high throughput players. She didn't question his call, she did what he wanted instantly, and it worked perfectly.

Now it was Tim's turn to act. As soon as her interrupt hit, he cast Rectify and stopped the buff from going off. No one should be stepping in the fire anyway, but if they did, he wanted them to take as little damage as possible.

A grin spread across his face as he thought about their last few moves. Together they managed to stop an attack and the buff. Not only that, but the group did it without wasting an extra interrupt. Now they might have one available down the stretch when they really needed it.

Behold My Power activated as the shapeshifter threw out five more coins. Everyone in their group saw the attack the first time it went off so they were ready to avoid the perils of the fire swamp. Their real problem was the original five landmines, and the patches they left behind hadn't disappeared yet. A few more casts, and they were going to start having trouble moving around the room.

It's only ten spots. Ten isn't so bad.

Cassie rotated the boss a little so the next set of coins might cover an area they'd already hit. It was the right idea, but he didn't think they would see another coin attack until after the first phase change. Things were going well after stopping the special attack and the buff, but when things felt easy, it meant they were about to get hit with the whammy.

The boss hit seventy-five percent health, and all hell broke loose.

ShadowLily disappeared, and so did the shapeshifter. Tim had no idea what was going on, but it didn't make sense for them to stay spread out so they could be picked off one at a time.

"Group up." They rallied to him, backs together, watching for any sign of attack.

Tim thought they might get off lucky and that this part of the fight would come down to ShadowLily kicking the shapeshifter's ass mano-a-mano while they waited around. He wasn't worried for her. Tim knew she'd win. He was scared to find out what was coming for them.

The circles on the floor left behind from the landmines pulsed, and the surface started to shift. As it cracked, an insectile head worked its way free. Moments later, a wasp hovered in the air in front of them.

Lorelei was on it, using her bow to bring the creature down, but soon the other circles were disgorging hellish flying creatures. The group had to scramble to try and bring them down before they were overwhelmed.

Normally a few wasps wouldn't be that scary, but these ugly things had two-foot-long stingers dripping green poison. The drips left little *hisses* of steam when they hit the floor. Tim didn't want to know what it would feel like to have that vile stuff injected into him.

JaKobi took the lead, casting a few of his Flame Walls to herd the wasps into a kill zone, while Lorelei hit them with volley after volley of an AOE attack. Tim added Flame Burst to the mix as Cassie sat back and watched all the excitement.

The tank blew on her nails before buffing them on her leather vest. "What? I'm not getting close to those things."

"Might not have a choice, depending on how many there are in the next round." Tim turned, taking in the room as he waited for ShadowLily to return.

Ash fell to the floor as the wasps burned away to nothing. The game AI was right about lighting things on fire. It was kind of fun. Not that he'd start running around burning every innocent animal he saw for shits and gigs, but if something was trying to kill him, Tim had no problem burning it to death.

Everyone's health looked fine. With all the wasps defeated, this was the time to regenerate some of their mana. Tim had the feeling when ShadowLily reappeared, she would need a Cleanse and a lot of heals, so having the downtime to recharge was a pleasant surprise.

The middle of the room started flashing red, and everyone scattered out of the way. Flames shot up from the floor in a raging inferno of swirling heat.

That was an insta-kill mechanic!

When the flames winked out, ShadowLily knelt on the floor, bleeding from several wounds as the shapeshifter stood over her gasping for breath. Tim only had eyes for his girlfriend and started casting Cleanse to stop the damage so he could heal her properly. What he should have been doing was calling the attack because the boss was stunned, and this was their time to do as much damage as they could.

"Attack!" Cassie roared.

For the next five seconds, the boss took one hell of a beating. Tim would've loved to be a bigger part of the action, but his attention stayed focused on casting Healing Orb on his girlfriend before reapplying Curse of Giving to keep Cassie in the fight. With everyone's health back in a decent place, they fell into the rhythm of the fight.

The shapeshifter threw out his coins. They avoided the fire and the lingering spots it left as best they could. Cassie managed to interrupt the boss's special attack. That meant only the ranged DPS had their interrupts left, and they would need at least one more to survive, probably both.

"Your deaths are inevitable," the shapeshifter roared, using its magic to push them to the side of the room.

JaKobi snickered. "I thought my death would come because I like eating cheeseburgers and washing them down with ice cream and brownies."

"Old age for me. I'm basically a saint," Lorelei added as she fired an arrow at the boss.

The arrow stopped a foot away from the shapeshifter and fell to the floor. Then he disappeared again. ShadowLily shouted something, some kind of instructions. Or maybe a warning? Tim couldn't make out the words. Everything around him was getting drowned out and muddy.

Holy shit, did he get sucked into one-on-one combat?

Sometimes the game seemed so unfair. It was hard enough being a healer. Having to face off against the boss solo was some next-level shit.

Thankfully his class centered around doing DPS. A more traditional healer might as well have cashed it in and hoped the next time they tried the fight, the RNG gods would be more forgiving and pick someone else. He didn't know how the rest of his group was faring without being up top, so Tim had to find a way to end this soon.

The one thing he didn't expect to see waiting for him as his vision cleared was a clone of himself.

The shapeshifter smiled and looked at its new skin. "Not much to look at, but powerful enough to end your life."

A blast of Divine Light launched from the shifter's hand. Tim threw himself to the side, hitting the deck hard. The first casts he made as he climbed back to his feet were Who Needs a Shield and Hex of the Shattered Beast. He didn't have a single doubt in his head that he'd be taking damage soon, and the more he could send back at the shifter, the better.

Plus, with his dog here, he didn't feel quite so alone.

Tim threw himself to the floor to avoid another attack and ate a blast of Divine Light as he returned fire. Cures of Giving and Curse of Sacrifice returned his health to one hundred percent, but the damage his first two spells did to the boss was like throwing raindrops in a river. To get out of this alive, he might have to get creative.

Rushing forward with his staff in hand, Tim swung the weapon at the shifter and felt gratified when it smashed into his side. He'd never used his staff as a direct weapon, and the creature wasn't expecting the attack at all. While the boss was distracted, Tim cast his highest single-target spell, Divine Light.

The shifter came at him with everything it had, and for the first time, Tim took damage in earnest. It was fucking weird casting spells and swinging his staff at himself. He'd wrestled with himself plenty in his life, normally over something trivial like going to a party on a school night instead of studying, but that was an internal battle.

This was something else entirely. It was like shadowboxing

in the mirror. Only if he lost this fight, he'd be dead instead of merely tired.

Thinking of the people counting on him to man up was what drove Tim to push as hard as he could to win. He couldn't let them down. It simply wasn't going to happen. He'd screwed up fights before but not this time. This time he was going to come out on top.

Hex of the Shattered Beast activated, and an unexpected force threw Tim to the floor. A DOT started ticking, and his health plummeted like a rock thrown in the ocean.

He was stunned. Then the flames rose around him. Tim screamed, but the fire didn't burn his skin as he expected. This must be it, the transition back to his friends.

Like that, Tim was standing back in the center of the room. He wanted to rejoice at rejoining the group, but everyone's health looked as bad as his. How long had he been gone? Was there something worse than the wasps coming out of the fire spots this time? He'd have to get with the others and compare notes after the fight. For now, all Tim had time to do was heal.

The boss's health was at forty-five percent, but Tim's was lower.

Healing rain fell from the heavens, interrupted only for a moment when Tim stopped casting Healing Storm and cast Mass Cleanse to free himself from the DOT and anyone else it might be affecting. As soon as everyone's health hit fifty percent, he turned off the waterworks and sent out three Healing Orb to cover the group in Hydrate. With the heavy lifting out of the way, Tim focused on Cassie as she battled the boss toe-to-toe.

"Lorelei, watch for the shoulder shake, and interrupt." Tim knew it was risky leaving JaKobi's interrupt until last.

The ember wizard had a way of getting lost in his rotation and not reacting to the calls as quickly as the others. Tim was putting a lot of faith in his friend and knew it would reward him when the right time came.

"I'm on it." The spirit archer growled as she dodged a burst of fire from the floor and sent a wave of arrows at the boss in response.

With the fight back in full swing, they were all waiting for the new wrinkle to show itself. It didn't take long for them to see the first thing that changed. Intermittent pillars of flame burst from random floor sections, and now the shifter threw out ten coins at a time. With the extra fire, additional coins, and the DOT on the tank, his healing was depleting his mana at a rapid rate.

Tim did his best work when things got dicey. Everything else fell away, and his casts came so rapidly his fingers hurt. They'd been able to handle ten wasps with ease, but twenty or more was asking a lot. Tim was pretty sure they could handle the flying invasion, but he hoped they didn't have to take the chance when they were this close to victory.

All they needed to do was stick with the plan.

At thirty percent health, a beam of light at ankle height swept across the room. They'd seen this trick before and knew how to beat it. If the developers added a second beam they had to duck under like last time, the fight would turn into a total shit show. They all handled the movement well, but it always made things more interesting. All it took was one little slip, and it was time to see Barbara.

Whatever happened to a good old-fashioned tank and spank or the ever-present loot pinata?

When the shapeshifter hit twenty-five percent health, Tim expected one of his friends to disappear into the void to face one more battle. Instead, the mechanic swept them to the edge of the throne room. Flames covered the far wall and started moving slowly forward. Tim watched the fire frantically, thinking it was fucked up that they would die because he must've missed some mechanic.

Then Tim saw a gap in the flames.

"Come on." He ran toward the gap. Then he noticed the next wave of flames coming toward them.

He sprinted now. "Hurry!"

Cassie didn't hesitate for a second. She picked up JaKobi and sprinted. The group made it through the first gap and ran for the next one. They zig-zagged their way across the throne room until they reached the boss. The shifter's shoulders started to shake as Cassie tossed JaKobi off her shoulder with a grunt.

"Make him hurt!" Cassie ran toward the shapeshifter.

Tim cringed, waiting for the boss's mega attack to go off. If he didn't die, he'd pick up the pieces as best he could, but if JaKobi didn't get his interrupt off, the fight was probably over. They were so close to ending this thing it would be a shame to die now.

A few seconds ticked past, and Tim opened his eyes. He wasn't in Barbara's waiting room so they must not have died. If they weren't dead, he had fucking work to do. JaKobi was lucky they were still in the middle of the fight, or he might have punched the mad bastard for cutting it so close. He was going to have to give him a new nickname after this.

Maybe the Heart Attack Kid.

The shapeshifter hit fifteen percent health and blasted all of them with an uncleansable DOT. This was it, the final race to the finish. Could Tim keep them alive long enough to win? He didn't hesitate for a second to start casting Healing Orb on the group.

When things got real, Tim slipped into a totally different

mindset. This was his time to shine—the moment he lived for. There was no way he'd let them down.

The battle took a turn against them as the uncleansable DOT stacked with the shapeshifter's normal attack. With both getting pounded by double damage, it was all he could do to stem the tide. Even when he used Cleanse to set the two melee fighters back to even footing, it lasted only a few seconds. The damage was piling up. Maybe he'd been a little too cocky.

If things didn't improve quickly, Tim would have to change stances and hope Cassie could handle losing his defensive protection.

The boss hit ten percent. The entire group's health was reeling.

Tim pulled the plug on his Way of the Boulder stance and flipped into Way of the River. He cast Hex of the Shattered Beast on Cassie and got back to doing as much damage as possible, now that his heals were going out to the entire group. The healing they received was less than it would have been if he flipped Way of the Boulder to each person as he healed, but now he was healing everyone at once without having to cast Healing Storm. It was cost-effective as long as Cassie didn't die.

By the time the boss hit five percent health Tim was casting Curse of Sacrifice on repeat. Every blast returned a small portion of his health because of his stance, so it eased the burden of the curse on his health pool. At this point, he didn't care if he ended the fight at one hit point. He wanted it to be over and for them to be victorious.

Small pulses of energy flashed from the shapeshifter. It was all unavoidable damage, and Tim cast Who Needs a Shield to try and buffer as much of it as he could. Instead of breaking down and casting Healing Storm like he normally would, Tim continued to focus on casting Curse of Sacrifice and Divine Light.

The extra damage was nice, but in his current stance, the

damage he was doing was the only thing keeping them alive. The only time he stopped damaging was when something forced him to cast a Cleanse.

The party's health was falling fast, but the shapeshifter's was falling faster.

With one final scream, the Shifter spun out of control. Its body turned into a version of Tim, then ShadowLily, then the king, before finally exploding in a burst of golden motes.

They did it. The fight was over.

CHAPTER FOURTEEN

"I really, from the bottom of my heart, love getting new fucking loot." Cassie watched as the motes rose into the heavens and the golden chest appeared.

JaKobi pulled her into a hug and kissed her. "Doesn't feel too bad saving the kingdom. I kinda like being a hero."

"He's not even bragging." Lorelei had a smile on her face that would have lit up the sky brighter than a full moon. "I really thought we were toast there for a second."

ShadowLily wrapped an arm around Tim's waist. "That's my man, coming through in the clutch."

Tim brushed some imaginary dust from his shoulder and moved toward the chest. "Biggest heroes get first dibs."

"And he's so modest." ShadowLily gave him a look that said he wouldn't be going first if he valued having sex any time soon.

Tim gave a nervous laugh. "You know, on second thought, maybe someone else should go first."

He didn't think his girlfriend would ever use sex as a weapon like that, but why take the risk? He knew he'd get a piece of loot regardless of what order he touched the chest. As awesome as getting his next piece of loot sounded, the real question was whether the king and Prince Desmond secured the stone. At this very moment, the Stone of Immoratis could be sitting in Eternia's hands.

It was one hell of a plan for them to sneak out and power up the goddess while the Blue Dagger Society fought against the shapeshifter. Thankfully they stalled the boss permanently, but if they hadn't succeeded, as long as they battled the creature long enough, good would have carried the day. Tim would have loved to have seen the shapeshifter's face when the king strode back into the throne room at the head of an army. Thankfully for the guards and their families, that particular scenario never played out.

"So who's going first?" Tim looked around the group, his eyes settling on ShadowLily's last.

She laughed. "You are. I just didn't want you to be so damn smug about it."

"Smug isn't something I'm known for. Maybe you meant to highlight one of my other wonderful qualities? Perhaps my loyalty to my friends, or that thing I do with the hot sauce that you like so much."

The mist slayer let out a little giggle. "Well, there is always that." She pushed him forward. "Show us how it's done."

If there was one thing Tim knew how to do, it was when to accept a gift. "Don't mind if I do."

It felt like it had been a while since he was first up, but it probably hadn't been that long. He didn't know why, but he felt nervous, like his piece of gear would set the tone for everyone else. Yep, that was it. He was altruistic by hoping he got awesome loot to inspire others.

What a load of shit. He just wanted something cool.

Reaching out and hoping for the best, Tim laid his hand on the chest.

Item Received: Arlen's Boots of Chaotic Intent

Arlen was a man of many passions. That tended to come out in the magical items he enchanted. With so many of them being unpredictable, his business fell to the wayside, but several of Arlen's magical items are still floating around the kingdom to this day. Equip any two or more pieces of Arlen's gear to receive additional bonuses.

+3 Endurance +4 Intelligence +6 Wisdom

The stats were nice, but he was giving up two dexterity in the switch, and his boots increased mana regeneration. While the additional protection and stats made the switch a no-brainer, Tim hated to see his dexterity go down at all. If he ever needed to use his daggers again, that skill was priceless. Not to mention it helped him dodge attacks. Something he was rather good at despite the game's insistence that he tossed his body around like a rag doll.

Maybe those flops and flails were cool parkour moves to the untrained eye. Oh man, he better not even think stuff like that or he'd pay for it later. The game had a way of keeping him grounded when he got too big for his britches, and normally it was death.

You're a good AI, a great AI, and clearly, I toss myself around as you say, Tim thought as he moved down to read the item's special ability.

Special Ability: Chaotic Intent

While Arlen's many skills ended up being a detriment as much as they were a boon, he sometimes made incredible enchants the world had never seen the likes of. Arlen often claimed all of the credit for his fantastic items, but what it really came down to was his lucky boots. Every skill used while wearing these boots will be subject to Chaotic Intent. The special ability will reduce or increase the effectiveness of each cast by between one and ten percent.

Tim knew everyone was watching him, but he was still trying to wrap his head around the item. The special ability made it risky. A negative ten percent roll at the wrong time might kill them, but a plus ten and he could be the group's savior when they should be dead. It was a risk. He'd have to watch his numbers and see how the item felt. If the boots trended more positive, they were a keeper. If the item kept his stats even, he might wait and see if he could track down another of Arlen's items of a larger benefit before replacing them outright.

Turning around to face the group, Tim let a smile crack his features so they knew the item was good. "I got a set-piece, but it's got a wonky special ability."

"How wonky?" JaKobi asked as he made his way forward.

Tim almost laughed out loud. For some reason, he saw himself inside Willy Wonka's chocolate factory. Finding Arlen's items was like when Charlie received the factory at the end of the movie. As long as it wasn't the Tim Burton version, the next item he found in the set would make the boots even more powerful.

"Plus or minus one to ten percent effectiveness on every skill used." It sounded weird saying it out loud, but Tim had the feeling that with a few more pieces of Arlen's gear, the odds of those numbers being on the plus side would be in his favor.

JaKobi patted him on the back. "That's pretty cool, man. Set items are the best stuff in the game."

Lorelei moved past them to put her hand on the chest. "But not until you get more than one."

Turning away from the chest to face the group, Lorelei wore a smile as well. "Necklace of Deadly Precision."

Tim leaned in closer to get a better look. "Are those dice?"

"Yep, but mine only increases my skills effectiveness," Lorelei smugly replied as she stuck out her tongue and blew him a raspberry.

That seemed a bit unfair unless the increases were lower. Tim put the thought out of his head. He didn't care who had the best items in the group, only that each item helped them win. Lorelei was an amazing DPS, and any extra damage she did would help all of them. So instead of feeling cheated about his item, he basked in the awesomeness that was their group.

"Don't go ruining my tough-guy vibe, but I'm happy for you." Tim hugged her.

ShadowLily laughed. "You've never had a tough-guy vibe. Trust me, that's part of what I love about you."

She moved away from Tim, reached out, and put her hand on the chest. She turned a moment later, looking like a college kid who received a free pizza sent to their dorm room. "Ring of the Silent Predator. Boosts my stealth and damage out of stealth."

"And the stats." The mist slayer put a hand to her forehead and pretended to swoon. "Are fucking unbelievable."

"Damn girl, save some for the rest of us." Cassie made her way to the chest, then stopped. "Hey, babe, why don't you go first."

JaKobi looked at her like it was a trap, but then he went for it.

Right before he reached the chest, she laid her hand on it instead. "I'll make it up to you later."

"Seems like a good deal for me." The ember wizard waited to see what his girlfriend pulled from the chest with a twinkle in his eyes.

Cassie turned back to the group. "Bracers of Strength, not the greatest title, but they do exactly what you think. Also, special ability to swap my strength with any other stat for five seconds."

"Whoa, so you could switch strength and dexterity for the ability to dodge more, or strength and willpower to recover more mana? That's a pretty handy talent." Tim thought about all the potential ways an item like that could be useful and was a little jealous.

Wisdom to Dexterity and activate Quick Feet, he'd run a mile before anyone else even took a step.

Cassie was beaming with pride. "I really do love it." She turned to JaKobi. "Time for you to put our gear to shame."

"If I don't get something epic, I get to do the thing with the butterscotch?" When Cassie nodded, he added, "Then I don't even care."

He slammed his hand down on the chest. "Come on, big whammy, give me the whammy!"

Tim laughed. He'd never seen someone try and get worse loot so they could have kinky sex.

JaKobi looked crestfallen as he turned. "Sun Staff of the True Believer, and it's fucking awesome."

"It's okay. I already placed the order for butterscotch." Cassie winked at him. "You know it's one of my favorite games too."

JaKobi gave a wild fist pump and pointed at Tim. "Are you ready to go? I have plans."

"Damn straight I am, but first, we have something to show them." Tim lined up next to his friend as the chest disappeared, and they got down with their new dance.

The ladies cringed as they watched, but the boys were having more fun than Kid 'n Play. They only stopped and looked up when someone at the back of the room cleared their throat. The real King Rasmus was standing before them with an amused expression.

"That was something you don't see every day," the king commented offhandedly to the prince.

Desmond was trying to keep a straight face but couldn't quite manage the task. "It certainly was."

King Rasmus moved toward the group, pulled a wooden box from his inventory, and presented it to them. "We didn't have time to make it out of the castle, but as promised, the Stone of Immoratis."

The king handed Tim the box, and he passed it to Cassie for safekeeping. "Thank you, King Rasmus, for living up to your word." He turned slightly. "You as well, Prince Desmond."

Desmond waved dismissively. "You did all of the hard work. It is we who find ourselves in your debt yet again."

"Along those lines, we should hold a great celebration to honor the brave adventurers." Rasmus looked thrilled by the idea. "The entire kingdom would celebrate."

Tim looked at the group for confirmation, and he felt confident enough with what he saw there to proceed. "As much as we'd love a big party, our quest for the goddess continues."

Bowing his head as if in mourning, Tim continued, "We've heard about the queen and think it would be much more fitting to honor her sacrifice. Without her steadfast will in the face of certain death, we wouldn't have the stone now, and Vitaria would have won."

The king looked sad as he thought about his wife. It must have been a real blow to be released from Cronos' grasp only to find out his wife was dead. Tim saw ShadowLily die once, and even knowing she could come back, it almost broke him.

"I can see the wisdom in your words." King Rasmus extended his hand. "You have my thanks, and each of you can pick an item from my treasury for your service to the crown.

Extra loot was always a great bonus.

Tim shook the king's hand and Desmond's. "If you ever need us, Liz at the Blue Dagger Inn can always get in touch with us."

Cassie tapped her wrist. "We have a goddess waiting. Let's get moving."

The king bowed to them. "When you finish with your quest in the desert, come and see me again. For adventurers with your talents, there is always work available."

"Then you will see us again shortly." ShadowLily returned

the bow. "How do we get out of here with all the doors locked?"

"I'll handle that." Rasmus winked at her. "Guards!"

The doors flew open so quickly it was like a tornado had burst into the room.

The king addressed the head of his guard. "See these adventurers returned to their carriage and safely back to Blue Dagger Inn."

"Yes, Your Majesty." The man saluted and motioned for them to follow him out of the throne room.

Tim couldn't believe it. After all their work, they finally had the stone and good news for Eternia.

CHAPTER FIFTEEN

Eternia was waiting for them by the fireplace in her room. It was funny how Tim could imagine their great victory so differently than from how it happened. There was no ceremony like at the end of *Star Wars*. No one was going to pin a medal on his chest. Instead, he knelt on one knee with the rest of his group right behind him.

While this moment didn't have the fanfare and the fluff, it was much more intimate. He saw the appreciation in the goddess' eyes, and it meant the world to him. This was a special moment. The tide of fortune was turning slowly in their favor. Soon the goddess would be back to full strength, and they could take the fight back to Vitaria.

Eternia had a way of looking at a person and knowing them as intimately as if they had been friends their entire lives. As he knelt in front of her, Tim hoped she could feel his gratitude. The quest she had sent them on was daunting, but it had also been rewarding.

The grin he was wearing as he met Eternia's eyes threatened to split his mouth at the corners. "We have retrieved the Stone of Immoratis and present it to you now."

Cassie stood, pulling the wooden box from her inventory. She moved forward with purpose and placed the box into Eternia's waiting hands. "I think you'll find this is what you've been looking for."

Eternia took the box and opened it slightly. A smile spread across her lips. "I can already feel my power returning. In a few days, I'll be strong enough to reactivate the portal network. A few days after that I'll be back to full strength, and our battle in the desert will continue."

Tim rose to his feet and felt the warm glow of a job well done spreading through him. This quest had taken everything they had, they even died, but in the end, they came out on top and delivered the stone. It felt great, and they still had rewards to claim. He could tell Eternia wanted some privacy so she could do whatever she needed to activate the stone away from their prying eyes.

"Will you be here in the morning to go over our next steps?" Tim knew she wouldn't miss the hint that he was trying to leave.

Eternia set the box down on the table next to her chair before standing and pulling Tim into a warm embrace. When the goddess released him, she moved to Cassie and the rest of the group.

When she finished showing her affection, Eternia returned to her seat. "I would think the five of you would be looking forward to a little downtime. Enjoy this moment, for soon all of Promethia will need your services again."

The goddess looked thoughtful. "As my power returns, I can already spot several locations and adventures where you could make a difference, but our first duty must be stopping Vitaria."

Ushering them from her room with her gaze, the goddess smiled warmly. "So go and indulge yourselves in life. For the next three days, your only duty is to do nothing but think of yourself, to recharge your energy for the fight that lies ahead."

"Wait, we're getting a vacation?" JaKobi clapped. "I can finally go to the library."

Cassie hooked her thumb at him. "This guy gets his first vacation in the game, and he doesn't think *beach party*. He thinks of going to the library."

"Is it wrong I was thinking about the forge?" Tim looked at ShadowLily for confirmation.

The mist slayer kissed him. "Of course not, as long as you start tomorrow. Tonight you're all mine."

"Sounds like I win twice on that deal." Tim couldn't believe his luck.

ShadowLily tugged his arm, pulling him from the room. "I'm also hoping to win twice."

"Oh snap!" JaKobi catcalled as they made their way toward the door.

They were about to leave when Tim jerked them to a stop. It didn't feel right that they could all celebrate, but Lorelei couldn't see Neema.

"Eternia, I know it's not my place to ask, but..." His voice trailed off as the goddess nodded.

Eternia stood from her chair once again and took Lorelei's hand in hers. "The portals will be active in three days. Enjoy your time with her."

It dawned on the spirit archer what Tim had asked for. She ran toward him and pulled him into a hug. "Thank you."

"Just looking out for one of my friends." Tim returned the hug and laughed as the goddess touched Lorelei, and she disappeared.

ShadowLily tugged Tim's arm. "That was some sexy stuff, mister."

"I do have my moments." He let himself be dragged out the door and into their private suite.

"Babe, I'm heading down to Joe's to get something to eat," ShadowLily announced right before the door closed.

Normally he would've been worried about missing a delicious meal, but he knew she wouldn't come back without something for him. He deserved this shower. He'd earned it in the throes of passion. Sometimes a good roll in the hay was better than a week's worth of cardio—okay, it was better than cardio all the time.

While he was in the shower was also the perfect time to hand in the last of his pending quests. The last thing he wanted to do was leave a big pile of quest clean-up for tomorrow. Tim had the feeling despite their need for a vacation, they wouldn't be on one as long as they thought. Adventures had a way of finding them.

Tomorrow, Tim would spend the day at the forge. He'd been away from Ironbeard's shop for way too long.

Part of him wondered if swinging the hammer would be easier now that he didn't have the strength of a six-year-old.

He pulled up his user interface and went straight to his quest updates. Despite the fact he earned this shower, if he were MIA for more than an hour, he would be in a lot of trouble.

Quest Complete: Veil of Madness

You've already received the only reward promised for this quest, the Stone of Immoratis. In his generosity, the king has offered you the choice of an additional item to show his appreciation for all you've done. Select your reward to complete the quest.

Tim pulled up the list of items the king offered them. It didn't take him long to zero in on something he wanted. With a single mental *click*, he selected the item, and it appeared in his inventory.

Item Received: Arlen's Bracelet of Balance

Now and then, the stars aligned when Arlen made an

item, and it came out perfect. Or in this case, downright spectacular. This bracelet increases the chance of obtaining a positive roll of Chaotic Intent by a small amount. It also looks pretty cool and comes with additional stats. +2 Endurance +4 Dexterity.

After all the mental wrestling he'd done about changing his boots out because of the loss of dexterity, Tim managed to secure an item that not only replaced the loss but increased the stat a little bit. It didn't do much for his main stats, but the special ability and the extra bonus to secondary stats he cared about made it an irreplaceable upgrade.

The king outdid himself.

The experience from the quest was something he'd almost forgotten about, but it moved his meter so close to the next level that turning in Eternia's quest should earn it for him. Was there a better feeling in the world than when a person worked hard to achieve something and got it? He didn't think so. The work and sacrifices behind the outcome were what made winning so special.

Working hard always paid off in the long run.

Quest Complete: Stone of Immoratis

You've retrieved the Stone of Immoratis, and the goddess is powering up. Don't worry. She didn't count your request for Lorelei against the favor she owes you. I'd think carefully about what you want before asking because you might never have this opportunity again.

This quest will remain marked as incomplete until you cash in on the favor. Until then, enjoy the gold and experience that you so rightfully deserve.

System Message: You have received twenty gold

System Message: You have gained a level.

"Ba-da-boom, ba-da-bing!" Tim cheered to himself in the shower.

Not only did he have a favor to call in from the goddess

when she was back to full strength, but he had one more stat point to put in place before his vacation started for real. Tim turned off the shower and dried off. Without a thought, he dumped it in strength. Every stat point was one closer to his goal of twenty.

Once dry, he equipped his armor and headed for the door. ShadowLily wasn't back yet, and he didn't have broken legs so he went to join her at the restaurant downstairs. If nothing else, he could help her carry the food back to their room.

It was a good thing Tim didn't wait because when he made it downstairs, there was a huge spread of food and everyone was celebrating together. Even King Rasmus and Desmond were there. It was the perfect ending to an epic quest.

"Long live the Blue Dagger Society!" Tim called, and they all cheered and *clinked* their glasses together before returning the toast.

LIST OF TIM'S CURRENT STATS AND SKILLS

"Tim" level twenty-two Hex Witch
   Primary Stats
   Strength: 17
   Endurance: 34
   Dexterity: 30
   Intelligence: 62
   Wisdom: 74
   Perception: 7
   Vitality: 5
   Revitalization: 5
   Luck: 8

Notable Gear
   Weapons
   Simple Dagger of Dexterity, +1 (X2)
   Greater Staff of Yin, +3 Endurance, +7 Intelligence, +7 Wisdom
   Orb of Concentration, +5 Intelligence +4 Wisdom

Armor

LIST OF TIM'S CURRENT STATS AND SKILLS

Circlet of Divine Wisdom, +1 Endurance +3 Intelligence +5 Wisdom

Shoulder Guards of the Spotless Mind, +1 Intelligence +2 Wisdom +1 to Perception, Vitality, Revitalization, and Luck

Hex Witch's Armament, +2 Endurance +2 Dexterity +6 Intelligence +8 Wisdom

Dragon Hyde Jerkin, +2 to all base stats, +1 to all secondary stats

Bearhide Wrist Guards of the Faithful, +1 Endurance +1 Wisdom, Special ability: Bear Necessities

Paul's Gloves of Mending, +7 Intelligence +4 Wisdom

Belt of Divine Inspiration, +1 Endurance +2 Intelligence +4 Wisdom

No That's Not a Brown Spot Leather Pants, +3 Endurance +2 Dexterity +4 Intelligence +3 Wisdom, Special Ability: Flee

Arlen's Boots of Chaotic Intent, +3 Endurance +4 Intelligence +6 Wisdom, Special Ability: Chaotic Intent any skills effectiveness will be increased or decreased by one to ten percent

Jewelry and Accessories

Arlen's Bracelet of Balance, +2 Endurance +4 Dexterity, Special ability to influence the outcome of Chaotic Intent

Wristband of the Faithful. +1 Endurance, ten seconds of double mana regeneration

Ring of Luminosity, +1 Endurance +2 Intelligence +3 Wisdom

Necklace of Hydration, +1 Endurance +2 Intelligence +5 Wisdom

Trinket of the Smiling Monkey, +1 to random stat

Skills

Hex of the Shattered Beast: Novice rank three

Appeal to the Goddess: Novice rank five

LIST OF TIM'S CURRENT STATS AND SKILLS

Curse of Sacrifice: Novice rank six
Night Vision: Apprentice rank one
Backstab: Apprentice rank four
Rectify: Apprentice rank four
Throwing Knives: Apprentice rank four
Sneak: Apprentice ran six
Disturbance: Apprentice rank five
Quick Feet: Apprentice rank five
Shadow Master: Apprentice rank six
Small Blades: Journeyman rank one
Snare: Journeyman rank one
Dodge: Journeyman rank six
Flame Burst: Journeyman rank six
Behold My Power: Journeyman rank seven
Who Needs a Shield: Journeyman rank seven
Divine Light: Journeyman rank eight
Healing Storm: Journeyman rank eight
Curse of Giving: Master rank one
Cleanse: Master rank one
Healing Orb: Master rank three

Stances
Way of the River
Way of the Boulder

Buffs
Weaken Undead: Journeyman rank two
Armor of Eternia: Journeyman rank seven
Attacks of the Faithful: Journeyman rank seven

Open Quests
The Stone of Immoratis

THE STORY CONTINUES

The story continues with book thirteen, SISTERS OF ETERNAL BLISS, coming soon to Amazon and Kindle Unlimited.

BOOKS BY BRADFORD BATES

Ascendancy Legacy

The Arena

Jar of Souls

Guardian of the Grove

Demon Stone

The Rising Darkness

Redemption

Ascendancy Origins

Rise of the Fallen

Butcher of the Bay

Night of the Demon

The Bozley Green Chronicles

Possessed

The Galactic Outlaws

Forced Compliance

Genetic Purge

Smuggler's Legacy

Fortune Hunters

Star Talon

Lost Signal

A Galactic Outlaws Story

The Marchenko Incident

Smuggler for Hire

Origin Ice

The Fairy of Salem

Witching Hour

The Wild Hunt

Standalone Titles

Crimson Stars

BOOKS BY MICHAEL ANDERLE

Sign up for the LMBPN email list to be notified of new releases and special deals!

https://lmbpn.com/email/

For a complete list of books by Michael Anderle, please visit:

www.lmbpn.com/ma-books/

CONNECT WITH THE AUTHORS

Connect with Bradford Bates

Facebook:
https://www.facebook.com/bradfordbatesauthor/

Twitter:
https://twitter.com/Freetheblizz

Website:
http://www.bradfordbates.com/

Connect with Michael Anderle

Website: http://lmbpn.com

Email List: http://lmbpn.com/email/

https://www.facebook.com/LMBPNPublishing

https://twitter.com/MichaelAnderle

https://www.instagram.com/lmbpn_publishing/

https://www.bookbub.com/authors/michael-anderle

ABOUT BRADFORD BATES

Bradford Bates is a full-time author, husband to an incredible wife, and father to four furry rescue dogs. He lives in sunny Phoenix, Arizona, trying to not melt in the oppressive heat of the summer. When he isn't busy writing the next book, you can find him playing video games and watching scary movies.

www.ingramcontent.com/pod-product-compliance
Lightning Source LLC
LaVergne TN
LVHW041812060526
838201LV00046B/1238